HorrorLand

# WEREWOLF VILLAGE

ENJOY A HAIR-RAISING HIKE IN WOLFSBANE FOREST.

GO WILD AT THE ALL-NEW WEREWOLF PETTING ZOO.

AND LAST BUT NOT LEASHED...
DON'T MISS OUR "SUNRISE SPECIAL":
WEREWOLVES EAT FUR FREE!

Spend One Day at HorrorLand and You'll Never Be the Same.

www.EnterHorrorLand.com

## GOOSEBUMPS HorrorLand™
### ALL-NEW, ALL-TERRIFYING

## GOOSEBUMPS®
### NOW WITH BONUS FEATURES!
**LOOK** IN THE BACK OF THE **BOOK**
FOR EXCLUSIVE AUTHOR INTERVIEWS AND MORE.

# DR. MANIAC VS. ROBBY SCHWARTZ

## R.L. STINE

SCHOLASTIC INC.
New York Toronto London Auckland Sydney
Mexico City New Delhi Hong Kong Buenos Aires

No part of this publication may be reproduced, stored in a retrieval system, or transmitted in any form or by any means, electronic, mechanical, photocopying, recording, or otherwise, without written permission of the publisher. For information regarding permission, write to Scholastic Inc., Attention: Permissions Department, 557 Broadway, New York, NY 10012.

ISBN-13: 978-0-439-91873-2

Goosebumps book series created by Parachute Press, Inc.

Goosebumps HorrorLand #5: *Dr. Maniac vs. Robby Schwartz*
copyright © 2008 by Scholastic Inc.

All rights reserved. Published by Scholastic Inc., *Publishers since 1920.* SCHOLASTIC, GOOSEBUMPS, GOOSEBUMPS HORRORLAND, and associated logos are trademarks and/or registered trademarks of Scholastic Inc.

12  11  10  9  8  7  6  5  4  3                    11  12  13/0

Printed in the U.S.A.                                          40
First printing, October 2008

# 3 RIDES IN 1!

# DR. MANIAC VS. ROBBY SCHWARTZ

"Ouch!" I swatted a mosquito on my neck. Too late. I could feel a trickle of warm blood under my fingers.

My hiking boots sank into the muddy ground. I heard a rustling sound in the bushes. Probably a killer coyote getting ready to bite my throat out.

How much do I enjoy these family camping trips?

How much would I like to have all my teeth pulled out by a crazed orangutan with rusty pliers?

"Robby, try to keep up!" my dad called as he led the way along the trail.

"Yeah, Robby," my brother, Sam, shouted. "Try to keep up!"

He hates camping, too. But he pretends he likes it. That's because he's the middle kid, so he has to try harder.

"Stop copying Dad!" I shouted.

"Stop copying Dad!" Sam repeated, like a stupid parrot.

"Give me a break," I moaned.

"Give me a break," Sam echoed.

"Give *me* a break!" my sister, Taylor, whined.

Mom and Dad laughed. She's seven. They think everything Taylor does is the cutest.

They even laugh when she burps. When Sam and I have a burping contest at the dinner table, Mom always gets angry and makes us stop.

How fair is that?

"Whoa!" I let out a cry as my foot caught on a fallen tree limb. I lost my balance, stumbled — and fell into the mud. My backpack landed hard on top of me.

I heard Sam and Taylor laugh.

"It isn't funny," Mom said. She says that a lot. She's the only one in our family who isn't a total joker.

"Sure it's funny," Sam said. "Robby is a superklutz."

"Superklutz! Superklutz!" Taylor chanted. She did a crazy dance around Mom and Dad.

Dad set down the tent and helped pull me to my feet.

"Hey — a new superhero for your comic strip," he said. "Superklutz. He trips and falls on the bad guys."

I rolled my eyes. "Ha-ha," I said. "See me laughing? How funny are you? NOT!"

4

My family always gives me lame ideas for my comic strip. I just ignore them. They don't have a clue how serious I am about my strip.

Dad tugged my backpack onto my shoulders. Then he rubbed his hand through my hair and messed it up.

My hair is light brown, almost blond. And I wear it long and wild. I just sweep it back with my hand. I never brush it.

I have a lot of hair. It doesn't even fit under a baseball cap.

I think that's why Dad is always messing it up. Because he's as bald as a bowling ball.

A few weeks ago, I drew a comic character for my strip who looked like Dad. I called him Pink Head. I never showed that one to Dad. He's kind of sensitive about having a big pink egg for a head.

I'm the only one who's blond and pale in my family. Sam and Taylor both have raven-black hair and deep, dark eyes, like Mom. They're both short, and Sam is a chubster. He hates it when I poke his belly and tell him it's just baby fat.

The sun slid behind some clouds. The woods grew darker.

Dad pointed up ahead. "Let's set up camp by those tall trees," he said. "There's grass there. It should be less muddy."

I brushed a swarm of gnats out of my face.

What's the point of gnats, anyway? I mean, do we really need them? I don't *think* so.

We found a nice clear space under the trees. Then we set to work putting up the two tents. Mom and Dad started to unpack the sleeping bags.

Dad took a long drink from a water bottle. Then he spit a gusher of water at me.

I ducked out of the way. "Nice try!" I shouted.

Mom gave Dad a shove. "Norman, give Robby a break."

"Do it again, Dad!" Sam shouted.

Dad laughed. "Hey, Robby, who taught you how to do the perfect water spit? I did — right? The Spritz Master!"

I rolled my eyes.

"Why can't anyone in this family ever be serious?" Mom asked.

I pulled out my laptop and sat down on my backpack. I balanced it on my knees and booted it up.

After a few minutes, I called to Dad. "I'm trying to upload my comic strip. But there's no network out here. How am I supposed to get online?"

"Why don't you try to enjoy the woods instead?" Mom asked. "This is a *camping* trip. Put that away."

I groaned. "It's so *boring* out here! Nothing but nature, nature, nature!"

Dad grinned at me. "Your mom and I *like* nature. Fresh air. The great outdoors . . ."

"You're both weird," I said.

He pointed to the trees. "You promised not to grumble, remember? The sun is going down. Go help your brother gather firewood."

I grumbled some more. Then I put away the laptop and trudged into the woods to help Sam.

I really wanted to work on my new comic strip. I've been drawing comics since I was seven. But my new supervillain is my best one ever.

*Dr. Maniac. The Totally Mental Maniac of Mayhem.*

Awesome, right?

I tripped again and banged my shoulder against a tree trunk. Leaves shook and shivered above my head. A chipmunk stood up and stared at me. Then it scurried into the woods.

*Dr. Maniac vs. Chipmunk Boy.*

That might work. Dr. Maniac forces a boy to eat a poisoned acorn and he grows into a giant chipmunk. Dr. Maniac decides to turn a *thousand* boys into chipmunks. . . .

I can't help it. I get these great story ideas everywhere I go. Even in the woods.

I stopped and glanced around. Where was the path? I was walking over a thick blanket of sticks and dead leaves. The tall trees blocked out the sun.

How far had I walked? I have a terrible sense of direction. I get lost in my own bedroom!

"Hey, Sam!" I cupped my hands around my mouth and shouted. "Sam? Are you here?"

No answer.

"Hey — SAAAAAM!" I shouted louder. "Where ARE you?"

A bird cawed loudly somewhere in the forest.

Then I heard footsteps. Behind me.

I spun around — and gasped as a figure stepped out from behind two trees.

"No! It c-*can't* be!" I stammered. "You — you're not *real*! I made you up!"

A grin spread over Dr. Maniac's face.

Yes. Dr. Maniac. The comic villain I created.

He walked up to me with that crazy grin on his face. He brushed back his leopard-skin cape. "I'll show you how REAL I am!" he shouted. "Eat this DEAD SQUIRREL!"

He raised his yellow-gloved hands. He held a decaying dead squirrel. Its eyes had sunk deep into its head. Patches of fur had fallen off its back.

"EAT it!" Dr. Maniac shouted.

I tried to move away, but I backed right into a wide tree trunk.

"You're *crazy*!" I cried.

Dr. Maniac shook his head. "I'm not crazy — I'm a MANIAC!"

He bumped me with his chest. It had a big gold M on it. "Now, eat it!" he demanded. "EAT it!"

And he shoved the putrid dead squirrel into my face.

8

# 2

Hope I didn't confuse you. That last chapter was just a comic strip I drew.

Sam and I were sitting in the back of our SUV. We hadn't gone camping yet. We were on our way.

Dad was driving the whole family to the woods. I was showing Sam my newest Dr. Maniac strip on my laptop.

"What do you think?" I asked. "The dead squirrel thing is good — right? Do you like it when Dr. Maniac shoves the disgusting squirrel corpse right in my face?"

"Yeah. Pretty cool," Sam said, staring at the screen. "But one thing I don't get. Who's the chubby little shrimp who goes camping with our family?"

"That's you," I said.

Sam punched my arm. "*No way* I look like that," he said.

"Ever look in a mirror?" I said.

"Ever take drawing lessons?" he shot back. "I'm almost as tall as you are!"

Trees whirred past us as Dad roared down the highway. He couldn't wait to get there. Mom and Dad love camping, and they drag us with them almost every weekend.

The only thing I like about camping is that it gives me new ideas for my *Dr. Maniac* strip.

Farms with grassy green fields rolled past. Taylor sat in the middle seat, clapping her hands to music from the radio. Mom kept pointing out every cow and horse. But no one paid any attention.

Sam read my comic strip again. "What if you go picking up firewood in the woods today and Dr. Maniac really *does* show up?" he asked.

"Robby," Mom called from the front seat. "I hope you'll put the laptop away and help out this time. You always make Sam and Taylor do all the work."

"Yeah. Join the family for once!" Taylor said. She turned around and stuck her tongue out at me. Her tongue was bright purple from the candy she was eating.

*Attack of the Purple Tongue!*

*Good name for a comic*, I thought. *What if a boy is at the dentist's office? The dentist messes up — and the boy's tongue falls out. The tongue starts to grow. It's very angry. It doesn't like being outside the mouth. The tongue ATTACKS!*

"Look at those sheep," Mom said, pointing out her window. "Are you two boys enjoying the beautiful scenery?"

"Sam, what do you think I should do next?" I asked. "Should I eat the disgusting, gross squirrel? Or should I try to escape? I can't decide which is cooler."

"Maybe both," Sam replied.

He is never any help. He doesn't like writing stories. He is a total game freak. He spends hour after hour playing *Battle Chess*. What a weirdo.

"I like Dr. Maniac's costume," Sam said. "He dresses like a total maniac! Red-and-blue tights with a gold M on his chest? Yellow gloves? White boots with yellow feathers all over them? And a leopard-skin cape? That's *insane!*"

"Yeah. He's a crazed nutcase," I said.

"*You're* the nutcase!" Taylor chimed in. "Why don't you draw a comic called *Robby Schwartz, the Maniac Older Geek Brother*?"

I reached over the seat and bopped her gently on the head.

"Maniac!" she screamed.

"Can't we talk about anything else?" Mom said. "Look at those interesting shrubs over there."

Interesting *shrubs*? Sam and I burst out laughing. "Good one, Mom!" I said.

Dad turned off the highway. We bounced along a gravel road until we came to a small muddy parking lot.

11

I stepped out the door into bright sunlight. The air smelled fresh and sweet. Two big red hawks glided round and round a grove of tall evergreen trees.

I packed my laptop carefully into my backpack. Taylor jumped out of the car. She ran up to me and stomped down hard on my sneaker.

"OWW! Why'd you do that?" I asked.

She shrugged. "No reason."

I limped to the back of the SUV. Time to unload our stuff.

We always take two tents, sleeping bags, cooking equipment, and lots of sweaters and extra clothes. We loaded up like pack animals and lugged everything into the woods. Not my favorite part of camping.

Actually, I don't *have* a favorite part of camping. But what can you do when your parents are total outdoor freaks?

We always follow the same dirt path through the trees. And after about twenty minutes, we came to a nice grassy clearing. Time to set up the tents and build a fire before the sun went down.

"I guess you want me to go find firewood," I said to Dad once the tents were set up.

"We all have our jobs," Dad said.

"Oh, yeah?" I said. "What's Taylor's job?"

"Being cute," Dad said.

Taylor stuck her tongue out again. Still purple. Real cute.

I set my pack with my laptop inside it down carefully at the back of my tent. Then I wandered across the tall grass to the trees to search for sticks and logs.

The air grew cooler as I stepped deeper into the shade. The wind blew my long hair around my face. A black-and-orange butterfly fluttered in front of me, as if it were leading the way.

*Wow,* I thought. *Here I am, alone in the woods, picking up firewood.*

*Just like in my comic.*

*This is the exact scene where I call to Sam, and he doesn't answer. And then Dr. Maniac pops out from behind the trees.*

And suddenly, I heard the bushes rustle. The scrape of footsteps. Moving toward me — fast.

"Dr. Maniac!" I gasped.

No. Not Dr. Maniac.

I stared as Sam stepped forward, his arms filled with twigs and sticks for kindling. "Robby — what's your problem?" he asked.

"You — you scared me," I stammered. I pushed my hair away from my face with both hands. "I thought it was Dr. Maniac," I said. "You know. Like in my comic strip."

Sam squinted at me. "Don't get weird," he said. "Don't start mixing up comics and real life."

My heart had been racing. It slowly returned to normal.

"Hey, Sam," I said. "Can you imagine what a messed-up place this would be if superheroes and villains were *real*? And they were always flying around in tights and capes?"

We both laughed. It was kind of a funny idea.

I bent down and started to pick some twigs up off the ground.

Sam had his arms full. He stood over me, watching. "Robby," he said, "how come you made your main character a villain? Why not make him a superhero instead?"

"I just think villains are a lot more interesting," I said.

A loud crackle from the bushes behind me made me jump. The twigs flew from my hands. "What was *that*?"

Sam laughed. "A squirrel, probably. Or a raccoon. We're in the woods, remember? Animals live in the woods?"

"Just joking," I lied. "I was trying to scare you."

I bent down to pick up the sticks I dropped.

And suddenly, my eyes went wide — and I let out a startled cry. "NO!" I screamed. "It's IMPOSSIBLE!"

"Nice try," Sam said. "But you didn't scare me. Try again."

"N-no. You don't understand," I stammered. "I'm not joking. Look."

A strip of cloth was caught on a tree branch. I pulled it off and held it up for Sam to see.

His dark eyes bulged. "Leopard skin?" he said in a whisper.

"Leopard skin," I said. "Just like Dr. Maniac's cape."

"That's stupid," Sam said. "What's that doing here?"

I stuffed the strip of cloth into my jeans pocket. "I don't know," I said. "But I'm going to find out."

I didn't tell Mom or Dad about the leopard-skin cloth. They probably would think that I put it there.

My family is always playing jokes on one another.

So sometimes it's hard to know what to believe and what not to believe.

We made a big campfire and cooked dinner on it. We all roasted hot dogs, except for Mom. She doesn't eat meat. So she grilled two soy burgers for herself.

They looked kind of green and gross. But she said *anything* tastes good cooked on a fire. Especially if you drown it in ketchup!

After dinner, we goofed around. Dad told some really lame jokes.

My favorite was about a boy who has a banana in his ear. Someone asks him, "Why do you have a banana in your ear?" And the boy answers, "I can't hear you. I have a banana in my ear!"

It's probably an old joke. But I never heard it before. And it cracked me up.

Taylor tried to make up some knock-knock jokes. But they didn't make any sense. Sam and I had to beg her to stop.

The moon floated low over the trees when we crawled into our tents to sleep. The night air was growing colder.

Taylor, Sam, and I were jammed into one tent. I snuggled deep into my sleeping bag. I tried to pull it up over my head, but it was too short.

I shut my eyes, ready for sleep. In the sleeping bag next to me, Taylor sang softly to herself.

"Shut up," I whispered. "How am I supposed to fall asleep?"

"You know I like to sing," she replied. "It's the only way I can go to sleep."

She's such a little freak. That's not the only weird thing she does. She also sleeps with her eyes *wide open.*

Is that disturbing or what?

I rolled over and turned my back to her. Outside the tent, I heard the *hoot-hoot* of an owl. A gust of wind rattled the whole tent.

I shut my eyes tight. And tried to clear my mind . . . not think about anything at all.

I drifted off for a short while. But something woke me up.

I sat up, blinking. My heart was pounding.

Someone was walking outside the tent.

I heard a low cough. The soft thud of footsteps on the ground.

Did I hear someone calling my name?

With a shiver, I pulled myself out of the sleeping bag. Sam and Taylor were asleep. Taylor made little whistling sounds with each breath.

I climbed to my knees and poked my head out of the tent.

The pale yellow moon glowed high in the sky. A dark line of clouds — like a snake — cut it in half. Clouds covered the stars. The air felt heavy and damp.

The footsteps were coming from the trees. I heard a voice speaking rapidly. What was it saying?

I was half asleep. Not thinking clearly.

I pulled on my sneakers and crept out of the tent in my pajamas. Maybe I was sleepwalking or something. I don't know. But I left our tents behind and walked across the clearing to the trees.

I followed the sounds into the woods. I had to know who was there. And why he was calling my name.

"It has to be Dad," I suddenly realized.

There was no one else camping near us. Of course — Dad. Playing one of his dumb tricks?

I stopped in the shadows in front of the trees.

And froze when I saw a figure slither out. Moving quickly, he slid toward me.

"Dad?" I called, my voice high and shrill.

Then I saw the cape — the leopard-skin cape — flutter in the wind.

Dr. Maniac stepped into the moonlight. And he was carrying a dead squirrel.

# 5

"You're *real*?" I said. My voice came out in a choked whisper. "It's impossible!"

"Eat this dead squirrel," Dr. Maniac said. His eyes bugged out. He grinned from ear to ear. His voice was low, from deep in his chest. The gold M on his shirt glowed in the moonlight.

"This is *crazy*!" I said. You don't exist! I made you up!"

"Eat the squirrel, Robby," he repeated. He raised the decaying squirrel in both hands. "Stop stalling. I want to see how brave you are."

"Me? Brave?" I choked out. "Are you crazy?"

"I'm not crazy — I'm a MANIAC!" he boomed. "Eat it! Eat the squirrel!"

He shoved it into my face.

*Ucccccch!* The sour smell poured into my nostrils. The squirrel fur was bristly and hard and scratched my cheeks.

My stomach lurched. I started to gag.

"Go ahead," Dr. Maniac said. "Show me how

brave you are. Are you the brave one? Or is it your brother, Sam?"

"Sam? You're crazy! NO WAY!" I screamed.

I staggered back. Away from the sick smell. Away from the hard, bristly body pressing against my skin.

I rubbed my nose. I wiped my face with both hands. Trying to rub away the horrible feeling of the dead creature.

Then I raised my eyes to Dr. Maniac. He held the squirrel in one hand and brushed his cape back with the other. He stared hard at me, studying me.

"Okay," he murmured. "Okay. Okay. Okay. I guess I'M the brave one!"

He raised the dead squirrel to his face — and CHOMPED into its belly.

Then he stood staring at me, chewing . . . chewing loudly. Chewing the dead meat.

He took another big bite. And chewed some more. He made a loud *gulp* as he swallowed the rotten squirrel flesh.

"Not bad," he said. "If you ignore the taste and the smell."

He held it out to me. It was mostly bones now. Most of the meat had been chewed away. "Want to try some? I saved you the head — the best part!"

I grabbed my stomach. *"Ulllllp."* I started to barf. Somehow I forced it back down. "I'm . . . going to be sick," I murmured.

21

"No time for that, Robby Boy," he said. "You're coming with me."

He tossed the squirrel into the trees.

"Huh? What are you saying?" I gasped. My stomach heaved.

"You failed the bravery test. But you're coming with me," he said. "You're going to help me destroy my enemy, the Purple Rage."

My mouth dropped open. "Now I KNOW you're crazy!" I exclaimed. "The Purple Rage is the *angriest* supervillain in history! He screams so hard, even his *breath* is deadly!"

Dr. Maniac shrugged his powerful shoulders. "So? Tell me something I *don't* know."

"Well, what can I do to help you?" I asked.

"You'll see," Dr. Maniac said.

Then he grabbed my arm and spun me around. He squeezed his strong hands over my shoulders and started to drag me away.

"No! Let GO! Let GO of me!" I wailed. "Let GO of me! Somebody — HELP!"

Sam squinted at the screen as he read the newest comic strip on my laptop. "Cool episode," he said. Then he laughed. "Robby, when Dr. Maniac grabs you, you look like a frightened geek."

Our friend Brooke nodded her head. "You got *that* right," she said. "I could *feel* your fear, Robby. Your drawing gets better and better."

It was Sunday afternoon. The three of us were upstairs in my room. We were huddled around my desk so I could show off the newest Dr. Maniac strip.

Yes. You probably figured out that the adventure in the woods wasn't real. It was just another comic strip.

Brooke brushed back her straight brown hair. She wears it very short with bangs across her forehead. Brooke is tiny and thin. She looks like a first-grader even though she's eleven, Sam's age.

She has sparkly blue eyes and a little turned-up

nose. Kids at school call her Elf, which she hates. She lives across the street. We have all been friends since I was four and they were three.

"Where did you get the idea for the Purple Rage?" she asked.

I shrugged. "Dunno. I guess I was in an angry mood. So I made up a new villain. I love villains. That's why I put so many of them in my comic strips."

I pulled out my big sketchbook and turned to my first drawings of the Purple Rage. I always do dozens of sketches of my characters in colored pencil before I scan in my finished art.

"See?" I held up some early sketches. "At first, I made his cheeks bright red. You know. To show how angry he was. But then I thought maybe that wasn't enough."

I flipped the page to show them the next drawings. These showed the Purple Rage in full costume, shaking a big purple-gloved fist in front of him.

"See? He's dressed all in purple," I said. "Purple cape, purple tights. He's always in a total rage, so his whole face is bright red. And then when he gets *really* mad, it turns purple."

"That's awesome," Sam said. He grabbed the sketchbook out of my hands. "Do you have sketches of *me* in here?"

I grabbed it back. "Why would I do sketches

of you?" I asked. "I already know what you look like."

"I *hate* the way you draw me," Sam groaned. "I look like a turtle."

"Then grow a few inches," I said, "and I'll draw you like a *tall* turtle!"

Brooke didn't laugh. "Short people can be superheroes, too," she said.

I tucked the sketchbook back onto its shelf. "For sure," I said. "I'll put you in the strip, Brooke. Wonder Elf! I'll draw you standing under a toadstool!"

I thought that was funny, but Brooke didn't laugh. Instead, she grabbed my hair with both hands and pulled as hard as she could.

I let out a screech.

"Wonder Elf Defeats the Mutant from the Hair Planet!" Brooke cried. She pumped her fists in the air.

I tried to smooth my hair, but it didn't go down. It bounced right back up.

"How was your family camping trip?" Brooke asked. "You just got back — right?"

"It was okay," I said. "You know. Lots of nature and stuff."

"Bor-rrrring," Sam groaned. He sat down at my laptop and started tapping away at the keyboard.

"Hey — what are you doing?" I asked.

"My computer crashed," he said. "Brooke and I want to play *Battle Chess*."

"Fine," I said. "No problem. Just use mine. Don't ask or anything."

"Thanks," Sam said, typing away. Brooke pulled up a chair beside him and sat down.

The opening game screen appeared. Bold music and floating chess pieces, all carrying guns. Sam and Brooke have to be the only two kids in America who play this game!

I hurried downstairs. I could see Mom and Dad through the front window. They were on their knees, planting seeds in the flower garden by the driveway. They sure love being outdoors.

I walked into the kitchen and pulled a bag of nacho chips from the cabinet. I grabbed a can of Coke from the fridge and started to the den to see if any good movies were on cable.

I was about to drop onto the couch when I heard a noise upstairs.

A loud *crash*.

And then a high scream of horror.

BROOKE's scream!

The Coke can fell from my hand and rolled across the den rug. I tossed the nacho chips onto the couch — and took off running.

I bolted up the stairs and ran down the hall to my room.

"Brooke — what's wrong?" I cried. "What happened?"

Someone had slid the bedroom window wide open. The curtains were blowing out.

Brooke stood by the window with both hands pressed against her face. Her eyes were wide with fright.

"What *happened*?" I repeated. "What was that crash?"

"S-Sam . . ." she stammered. She pointed to the open window. "Robby — Sam is GONE!"

A few minutes later, Mom and Dad were staring at Brooke, shaking their heads. Their hands were still dirty from the garden. Dad had a wide dirt smear across his sweaty forehead.

"I *am* telling the truth!" Brooke screamed. "Would I make something like this up?"

Dad waved both hands in front of him. "*Shhh.* Calm down. Everybody calm down."

"Did you call 911?" Mom asked. She folded her arms around her chest. I could see how scared she was. Her chin was trembling.

"Yes. The police are on their way," Dad said.

I sat next to Brooke on my bed. I kept staring at the open window. Brooke's story rolled through my mind again and again.

Dad wiped his forehead with his shirtsleeve. "Tell us again," he said to Brooke. "Start at the beginning. Think hard, Brooke. Tell us what really happened."

"I already told you what really happened,"

Brooke insisted. Her voice cracked. She was breathing hard.

"But — how can we believe —?" Mom started.

Brooke interrupted. "I swear!" she cried. She raised her right hand as if she were taking an oath.

"Tell us again," Dad said softly.

Brooke took a deep breath. Then she started talking in a trembling voice.

"Sam and I were playing *Battle Chess* on Robby's laptop. We heard a noise at the window. We turned around — and Dr. Maniac flew into the room."

Still hugging herself, Mom squinted hard at Brooke. "Dr. Maniac? Robby's comic character? You're telling us a comic character flew in the window?"

Brooke swallowed hard. "Yes. He landed right in front of us. He grabbed Sam and pulled him off his chair. I . . . I tried to save him. But . . . I wasn't fast enough. Dr. Maniac dragged him across the room. And then he *flew out the window* with him!"

Brooke started to sob. Her whole body shuddered.

Dad stepped forward and patted her shoulder to calm her. His hand left a round dirt smear on her sleeve. "Okay. Okay," he whispered.

Mom started pacing back and forth. "Brooke, Robby made up Dr. Maniac," she said. "He's a comic strip character. You *do* realize he isn't real?"

Brooke let out a sob. She wiped her wet cheeks with her hands. "I know you don't believe me," she choked out. "But he was real. He was here. And . . . and he took Sam with him."

"But, Brooke — that's impossible," Mom said. She leaned over Brooke. "Don't be afraid to tell us what really happened. Tell us the TRUTH!"

"Whoa — wait!" I cried. My heart skipped a beat. I stared at something on the floor in front of the open window.

I jumped off the bed, crossed the room, and picked it up. Two feathers. Two yellow feathers.

"Mom! Dad!" I shouted. I held up the feathers. "Dr. Maniac has yellow feathers on his boots," I said.

They both stared at the feathers. Brooke jumped off the bed, strode over to me, and took the feathers from my hand. "I told you," she whispered. "I told you. . . ."

Mom opened her mouth to say something.

But a noise downstairs stopped her. Loud thuds on the front door.

"Police!" a deep voice shouted. "Police! Please open the door! We found your son!"

"Oh, thank goodness!" Mom cried.

"They found him!" Dad exclaimed.

The four of us went running to the bedroom door. We made a traffic jam of arms and legs as we all tried to squeeze out the door at the same time.

Mom and Dad practically flew down the stairs. Brooke and I followed close behind.

I was gasping for breath as Dad pulled open the front door.

I stared at two black-uniformed police officers. They stood on the front stoop *with a boy I'd never seen before*!

Mom let out a cry. Her eyes bulged as she stared at the boy. He was tall and athletic looking, with curly brown hair, green eyes, and freckles on his cheeks.

"You're not Sam!" she yelled.

"I told them," the boy said. "My name is Jerome."

He rolled his eyes. "How come no one ever believes kids?"

"This isn't your son?" one of the officers asked.

Mom and Dad shook their heads.

"Where do you live?" the officer asked.

"On Brentwood," Jerome said. "Near the old library. My bike had a flat tire, and I was trying to walk home. That's when you stopped me."

"Take Jerome home," the officer told his partner. "Sorry, son." He turned to my parents. "I'm Officer Rawls. I'm real sorry about the mix-up. Let's go inside and straighten this out."

So we all trooped into the living room. The four of us sat on the edge of the couch. Officer Rawls leaned against the mantelpiece and took notes on a little pad.

Brooke began her story. But before she could get very far, the door opened and Taylor stepped into the room.

"I'm back from Patsy's!" she called. Then she saw the police officer — and stopped with a gasp. "What's up?"

"Sam is . . . missing," Mom told her. "Come here. Sit down with me. Brooke is going to tell the officer what happened."

So Brooke told her story all over again. By the time she finished, Officer Rawls had his cap off. He was scratching his short brown hair and blinking his eyes a lot.

Taylor walked over to Brooke. "Hel-lo," she said. "Are you and Sam playing a practical joke on us?"

As I said, our whole family likes to play jokes. Except for Mom, of course. So, naturally, that's the first thing Taylor thought.

"It's not a joke," Brooke whispered. Tears rolled down her cheeks again. "Really. Not a joke."

Taylor went pale. Her mouth dropped open. She stared hard at Brooke.

Officer Rawls placed his cap back on his head. He glanced at the little notepad in his hand. Then he turned back to Brooke.

"Brooke, please listen to me," he said softly. "I want you to think long and hard about this. You can see how upset Sam's family is. I want you to think about what happened up in Robby's room. And then tell it one more time."

Brooke let out a long sigh. Then she began telling her story again.

I couldn't sit still. I felt sick. My stomach was bubbling and churning. I kept picturing that open window. And I kept seeing my little brother's pudgy, smiling face.

Would I ever see him again?

I wandered into the den. I heard voices. The TV was on. A talk show my mom likes. It stars this big man with bright red hair that stands straight up on his head. Red Martinson.

I hate Red Martinson. He laughs at his own

33

jokes. He thinks he's a real riot. Mom thinks he's cute.

I reached for the remote to turn off the TV.

"So tell me," Martinson was saying to a guest, "how do you feel about things now?"

I let out a sharp cry when I saw the guest. The remote fell from my hand.

"I — I can't believe it!" I gasped.

I was staring at the Purple Rage! Red Martinson's guest was *my comic character* — the Purple Rage!

"How do I *feel* about things?" the Rage boomed. "I'm ANGRY! Know what really PINCHES my PIANO? *Everything!* I'm angry about EVERYTHING!"

His face turned as purple as his costume. His eyes were red and looked like they were about to pop out of his head.

"I'm ANGRY!" he shouted, and thumped his big fist on Red Martinson's desk.

"Most of our viewers won't believe you're real," Martinson said. "Do something super to prove you're the real deal."

"That BURNS my BUBBLE BLOWER!" the Rage screamed. "That makes me even ANGRIER! How could I be on TV if I'm not REAL?"

Then his face turned an even darker purple. Only a supervillain could turn *that* purple.

I gaped at the screen in disbelief. The Rage? Real? How could that *be*?

*Mom and Dad have got to see this!*

Breathless, I spun away from the TV. I ran back into the living room. Brooke was still telling her story. Officer Rawls was writing in his little pad.

I ran up to Mom and Dad. "Hurry!" I screamed. "In the other room! On TV!"

I pulled them toward the den. "It's my *other* comic character!" I cried. "You'll see! It's the Purple Rage! For *real*!"

They followed me into the den. I pointed to the TV.

"So what plans do you have for the future?" Red Martinson was asking.

"I'm glad you asked that question," the guest replied.

"Huh?" My mouth dropped open. Where did the Purple Rage go?

The guest was a white-haired man in a gray suit with a red necktie.

"That's Congressman McCloo," Dad said. "Robby, why did you pull us in here to see Congressman McCloo?"

# 9

My whole body was shaking. I stared at the screen. How could the Purple Rage disappear like that?

Mom rested her hand on my shoulder. "Robby, we know how upset you are," she said softly. "We know how much you care about your brother. But don't make it worse by making up crazy stories."

"But — But — But —" I sputtered. My brain was spinning. I couldn't speak.

Officer Rawls said he had to leave. He told us all to stick around. He said he would send his Crime Scene people to study the yard and the whole house. He promised he'd come back.

Mom and Dad went to Taylor's room to comfort her.

I pulled Brooke aside. "No one believes me," Brooke said, her voice cracking.

"No one believes me, either," I said. "But I know I'm not crazy. The Purple Rage was on TV. I saw him."

Brooke shook her head. "Maybe we *are* crazy. I mean, comic characters coming to life?"

I started to the front door. "Are you coming with me?" I asked.

She held back. "Huh? Where?"

"To the TV station," I said. "The Rage might still be there."

"Huh? The TV station? Robby, do you know where it is?"

"Yes," I said. "Remember? Our school went there last year to be on that kids' show?"

I pulled open the front door. Bright sunlight poured over me. "Are you coming or not?" I asked Brooke.

She thought for a few seconds, biting her bottom lip. "Okay," she said. "Let's go."

We took a bus to the Middle Meadows Mall. The WSTR-TV station was in a big green-glass building behind the mall.

Brooke and I stepped up to the green-glass door at the front. I pushed the bell.

The door buzzed. I pulled it open, and we walked into the reception area.

A blond-haired woman with bright orange lipstick sat behind the front desk. She wore a black business suit with a crisp white blouse. She had a sparkly starfish pin on her jacket.

WSTR is the "Starfish" Station. Don't ask me why.

My throat felt tight as I hurried up to her desk. And my hands were sweaty. I tried to brush down my wild and woolly hair to look more businesslike.

"Can we see Red Martinson?" I asked.

She studied me, then Brooke. "Do you have an appointment?" she asked.

I shook my head. "No. But it's really important," I said.

"We just want to ask him one question," Brooke said.

"Are you with your school newspaper?" the woman asked. She tapped a pencil on her desk.

"Uh . . . yes," I lied. "We want to interview Mr. Martinson for our paper."

"Well, you need an appointment for that," the woman replied.

"But —" I started. "I —"

"Was the Purple Rage here?" Brooke asked. "We just want to know if the Purple Rage was on his show."

The woman stopped tapping her pencil. She took a clipboard and ran her eyes down the top page. "Is he a chef? You might want to try the cooking show."

I let out a sigh. "You don't understand," I said. "He isn't a chef. He's a supervillain. I thought I made him up. But I saw him on TV. So maybe he's real. And if he's real —"

She squinted at me. "Are you making any sense? I don't think so."

I heard someone coming down the metal stairway right behind the reception desk. "Hey!" I cried as Red Martinson stepped out.

He wasn't dressed like he was on his show. He wore jeans and a black-and-red T-shirt that said CLEVELAND ROCKS. His red hair still stood straight up like an evergreen tree on his head.

He waved to the receptionist and started to the front door. But then he suddenly stopped and turned around to face us.

"Hey, I like your hairstyle, kid!" he said to me. He laughed. "Are you *copying* me?"

"Yes," I blurted out. "I mean, no. Mr. Martinson — we came to see you."

"Sorry," he said, "I left my autographed photos up in my dressing room. Can you come back? I'm in a rush." He pulled open the front door.

Brooke hurried after him. She grabbed his arm. "Was the Purple Rage just on your show?" she asked.

Martinson nodded. "Yes," he said. "At first I thought it was a joke. But he proved he was really a supervillain, so I put him on the show. Did you enjoy my interview?"

My heart started to pound. "Where *is* he?" I cried. "Is he still here? Where did he go?"

Martinson shrugged. "He had to fly somewhere," he said. "He went up to the roof to take off."

I didn't wait. I spun around — and ran. I brushed past the startled receptionist. I grabbed the metal banister and began running up the winding staircase.

"Stop!" she screamed. "Hey — stop! You can't go up there!"

My shoes clanged on the metal stairs. I heard Brooke running right behind me.

Where were we headed? Could we get to the roof from here? Was the Purple Rage still up there?

"Stop!" the receptionist screamed. "Security! Security! Stop them!"

# 10

I reached the second floor and kept climbing. The stairway straightened out. The stairs were concrete up here.

I could hear the heavy thuds of men's shoes behind us, coming up fast.

"STOP!" a man yelled.

"Security! Stop right there!"

Their angry voices echoed in the narrow hallway.

My chest felt about to explode. My legs ached. But I kept climbing, taking the stairs two at a time.

The third floor went by . . . and then the fourth.

Gasping for breath, I glanced back. "Brooke?"

No. Not there. She had been right behind me. Did one of those security guards grab her?

"Brooke!" I shouted. "Brooooooooke!" My cries echoed down the stairwell.

No reply.

My legs felt like heavy weights. My chest and side throbbed with pain. But I kept pulling myself up the steps.

"Stop now!"

"You can't get away! Stop running!"

The voices boomed close behind me.

Finally, I reached the top of the stairs. A broad yellow door stood at the end. I lowered my shoulder — heaved — and shoved it open.

With a gasp, I stumbled out into bright sunlight.

I fell onto the flat tar-papered roof. Landed hard on my knees.

Blinking in the light, I saw a blur of purple.

Just a brief flash. A one-second glimpse of a purple cape.

"WAIT!" I choked out. But my voice creaked out in a whisper.

The Purple Rage. It HAD to be him!

I jumped to my feet and staggered to the edge of the roof.

"Wait!" I screamed, a little louder this time.

I stumbled to the edge of the roof. Leaned over the side to see the Purple Rage.

"Whoa!"

I leaned TOO FAR!

It happened so fast. One second I was leaning out over the edge. And the next second the roof seemed to slide out from under my feet — and I was *falling*.

# 11

The buildings soared past me in a gray blur. The powerful rush of the wind chilled my back.

I fell so fast I couldn't hear my own scream.

Down . . . down in a bright blur.

No time to ready myself for the crash and the burst of pain that would end my life.

And then . . . *THUD.*

I hit hard. Pain shot through my arms, my neck, my back.

My head bounced up. The sky appeared to wrap itself around me like a blue blanket.

No. Purple. A purple blanket gripping me tightly.

And then a red face with a grim, tight-lipped expression.

Huh?

It took me a moment to realize that I hadn't hit the ground.

I was still in the air. Held up in the air. By the Purple Rage!

Yes! One arm under my legs, the other under my shoulders. Lifting me to the sky.

His cape was fluttering noisily in the wind. His dark eyes gazed straight ahead, then down as we started to descend. His powerful arms held me tightly against his massive purple chest.

The Purple Rage had swooped up and rescued me.

He floated to the sidewalk, cape fluttering behind him. He set me gently on my feet.

I was shaking so hard, I dropped to my knees. I knew my hair was standing straight up, wild around my face. I swallowed again and again, struggling to catch my breath.

The Rage pulled me to my feet. He held me up by my shoulders. His eyes burned into mine.

"Know what PADDLES my PANCAKES?" he boomed. His voice was so loud and deep, it made pigeons squawk and fly off the sidewalk. "Kids who fall off buildings! That puts me in a RAGE!"

"S-sorry," I stammered.

"Were you CHASING me?" he bellowed.

"No," I choked out. My heart was still hammering in my chest. "Not exactly."

I stared back at him. Was I *dreaming* this?

This wasn't a comic strip. This was real life. But there he was in front of me. His purple gloves held me by the shoulders. His eyes glared at me angrily.

*A character I created!*

"I — I need your help," I said, finally finding my voice. "My brother, Sam, is missing. I think Dr. Maniac took him."

The Purple Rage tossed back his head and uttered an angry roar. His eyes blazed red like fire, and he curled his hands into big fists.

"MY SWORN ENEMY?" he roared. "You say your brother has TEAMED UP with MY SWORN ENEMY?"

"No. That's not what I said," I replied.

But he roared like a furious beast again and drowned out my words.

"Listen to me —" I begged.

But he lifted himself off the ground. He spun around and *kicked* a store window with the toe of his purple boot.

I ducked as the glass shattered and flew everywhere.

The Rage kicked out a few more store windows. Then he turned back to me, his big chest heaving.

"How could your brother team up with that MANIAC?" he screamed. "I heard that Dr. Maniac teamed up with the SCARLET STARLET!"

"I — I don't know," I stammered, backing away.

The Scarlet Starlet? I drew her in my very first comic strip. Was *she* real, too?

I took a deep breath. "Are you going to help me?" I asked.

That sent him into another rage. His face turned

as purple as his costume. He grabbed the front of my shirt and lifted me off the sidewalk.

"Dr. Maniac sent you to spy on me — didn't he!" he boomed. His hot breath burned my eyebrows.

"No — no —" I said.

"LIAR!" he screamed.

He gazed up to the top of the building. "Wonder if I could toss you back up to the roof," he said.

"No — please!" I begged.

His fist tightened on the front of my T-shirt. He raised me above his head.

"Please — I only want your help," I wailed. "Don't throw me. Don't —"

I glanced around. Wasn't there anyone around to help me?

No. The street was empty.

"Looking for your friend Dr. Maniac?" The Rage cried. "Sorry, kid. He's too late to save you!"

He pulled back his arm — and *heaved* me with all his strength.

"NOOOOOOOO!" I screamed again as I went flying up to the sky.

# 12

My scream caught in my throat.

I couldn't breathe. The wind rushed too hard against my face.

I sailed straight up, my arms and legs thrashing.

I shut my eyes — and slammed hard into the side of the building.

*THUDDDDDD.*

My breath shot out in a *whoosh*. Pain swept over my chest. I choked and gasped for air. I kept my eyes shut and waited to die.

I counted to myself. One . . . two . . . three . . .

On three, I felt another hard *THUD*. I opened my eyes. And saw the red-faced supervillain staring at me.

The Purple Rage had caught me. He saved me again.

As he flew, he held me in front of him like a loaf of bread.

"Changed my mind, kid!" he shouted. "But it was good to see the old arm is still in shape. I could probably throw you to the next town."

"Uh . . . you're not going to — are you?" I asked.

He floated to the ground and set me down again. I bent over, grabbed my knees, and waited for my breathing to return to normal.

I tried to brush down my hair with both hands. But it sprang right back up. After today's adventures, I knew it would probably *never* come back down.

"Does this mean you'll help me find my brother?" I asked.

The Purple Rage nodded. "I will make it my mission. I cannot leave him in the hands of my sworn enemy."

"Awesome," I said.

"Yes, I AM awesome!" he declared, sticking out his big chest. "Do you know what really SNAPS my SHORTS? When other people tell me how awesome I am. Because I ALREADY KNOW IT!"

He grabbed a lamppost and bent it in two.

"Sorry," I murmured. "This . . . this is all so totally weird."

He squinted at me. "Weird?"

"Yes," I said. "Do you know that I *created* you?"

"NOOOOOOOO!" The Rage bellowed furiously. "YOU LIAR! I was created by a SCREAM from the mouth of the ancient god THOR!"

48

Before I could move, he grabbed me up with both hands. Holding me in front of him, he took off.

The wind blew against my face. Behind me, I could hear his purple cape snapping against the air. He soared higher, above the cars, above the buildings.

"Where are we going?" I screamed into the wind. "What are you doing?"

We flew toward the sun, into blinding white light.

I shielded my eyes with one hand. I tried not to look down, but I couldn't help it.

Far below us, a freight train rolled by on the North Hills tracks. It looked like one of those toy trains people set up in their basements. The buildings all looked like dollhouses.

"Please —" I begged.

Why was he so angry? What did I say to put him in such a rage?

Then I remembered — he was ALWAYS in a rage!

We neared the edge of town, and he suddenly swooped lower. A building came into view, hidden by tall evergreen trees.

It was a round stone building, shaped like an igloo. No windows. A low door in the front.

The building was completely surrounded by trees. Was it his hidden fortress?

I hadn't created a hidden fortress for him. I

hadn't created *any* of this. It was all happening without me. Beyond my control.

We dropped lower. I ducked my head as the Purple Rage roared into the open door. It was like a huge dark cave inside. We flew down . . . down. . . . The air felt heavy and wet.

I blinked hard, waiting for my eyes to adjust.

He dropped me onto my feet. I watched his cape settle behind him. He swept back his dark hair with both gloved hands. Then he pulled off the gloves and tossed them against the wall.

"Know what really TWEAKS my TUTU?" he shouted. "Dead leaves in my hair. How am I supposed to FLY with LEAVES in my perfect hair?"

"Dunno," I muttered. "Where are we?" I asked in a tiny voice.

He didn't answer. He moved to the wall and began clicking on lights.

I glanced around. We stood in a large underground cavern. The walls were solid stone.

The room was filled with camera equipment and spotlights. I saw a table filled with computers. Two TV cameras stood side by side next to a microphone on a long pole.

"Is this like a TV studio?" I asked.

The Rage didn't answer. He was busy fiddling with the computers. He typed frantically on one keyboard, then moved to another.

Then he pointed a TV camera at a glass case against the wall.

Something moved inside the big case. I walked over to it and gazed through the glass. Dozens of dark, spiny creatures crawled all over each other.

"What are those?" I asked, pointing.

"Scorpions," the Purple Rage answered.

"You keep a huge glass case filled with scorpions?" My voice came out shrill and tight. "But — what do you do with them?"

"You'll see," he murmured. He began moving lights toward the case.

I watched the scorpions sliding, crawling, scraping, snapping their claws at each other.

"They look hungry," I said.

A strange unpleasant smile spread over his face. "I'm going to feed them in a minute," he said.

"What do you feed them?" I asked.

He tossed back his head and laughed. "You," he said.

# 13

"But — but —" I sputtered. "You said you were going to help me find Sam."

He turned some dials on a big control board. Red lights flickered. Machines started to hum.

"I shall keep my promise," he said. He turned to me. "Know what really HONKS my HORSE?"

"No. What?" I said, unable to take my eyes off the scrabbling, snapping scorpions.

"People who get tense about me keeping my PROMISES!" he screamed.

He pulled his arm back and smashed his fist into the wall.

The wall cracked.

Muttering to himself, he dusted off his hands. Then he strode over, picked me up, and set me down in front of a TV camera.

"Stand there, kid. Don't move," he said.

"No problem," I whispered. "What are you going to do?"

He punched more keys on the computers. "I'm

going to interrupt all TV channels and Web sites in the city," he said. "Everyone will have the pleasure of watching the world's best-looking supervillain — ME!"

I didn't say a word. I didn't want to make him smash the wall again. I just wondered if he really planned to help me find Sam.

He stepped behind the camera and raised the lens a few inches. Then he moved in front of it. He stuck out his chest, swept back his cape, and cleared his throat.

"Hello, everyone. I am the Purple Rage!" he announced. He motioned to me. "And this is a kid named . . ."

He thought hard, gazing into the camera. Then he turned to me. "What's your name, kid?"

"Robby Schwartz," I said.

He waved a fist at me. "Is your dad Bucky Schwartz, the guy who owns the dry cleaners on Spring Street? Last time I brought my tights in, he shrunk them."

"No. My dad is Norman Schwartz," I said. "He's a lawyer."

The Rage turned back to the TV camera. "Sorry to interrupt your day, everyone," he said. "But I want you to watch me as I drop Robby into a seven-foot-tall case of stinging scorpions."

"Huh?" I gasped. "This is your plan for *helping* me?"

He moved his face up close to the camera lens.

"Let this be a warning to Dr. Maniac," he boomed. "And to anyone else who dares to challenge the Purple Rage!"

Then he grabbed me under the arms and lifted me off the ground.

"Whoa — wait!" I cried. "What about your promise? Is *this* your plan to help me find my brother?"

"Of course," he said. "When your brother sees you are about to be *stung* to death by these scorpions, don't you think he'll escape from Dr. Maniac and come to rescue you?"

"Uh . . . maybe there's a *better* plan?" I cried.

The Rage didn't reply. Instead, he raised me high above his head — and tossed me into the glass case.

# 14

I landed in a sitting position. Scorpion shells squished and crackled under me.

Before I could move, scorpions rolled their shiny dark shells over my legs. The creatures never stopped moving. They felt warm and dry and prickly against my skin.

I struggled to stand. But I slid and slipped on the wriggling hard bodies.

I cried out as a scorpion scrabbled over my waist. I tried to swat it off me. Lost my balance. And fell onto my back.

As soon as I was down, they swarmed over me. Their shells clacked and bumped as they covered me. Pincers swiped the air, snapping wildly.

"Ohh, help," I muttered.

And then I remembered two words that sent a cold shudder down my body: *scorpions STING!*

Yes. One sting from a poisonous scorpion could KILL.

So far, they were climbing over me, covering me. Crawling and snapping.

One sting! Just one . . .

Carefully pulling a scorpion off my chest, I struggled to my knees. I pressed my hands against the front of the glass case.

On the other side of the glass, I could see the Purple Rage. He stood in front of the TV camera. He kept pounding his chest with his fists, talking away.

"Get me out of here!" I shouted. But the glass muffled my voice. He didn't seem to hear.

Or care.

*Why didn't I create some HEROES?* I asked myself. *Why did I only create VILLAINS?*

*"Ow!"* I pulled a prickly scorpion out from under the back of my T-shirt.

Two scorpion pincers snapped at my arms. All around me, it sounded like scissors snapping . . . snapping . . . snapping.

One sting, and I was dead meat.

Even if Sam was watching this somewhere on TV . . . even if he was somehow able to escape from the clutches of Dr. Maniac and come to my rescue . . . he'd be too late.

I knew I had to break out of the case. The Purple Rage wasn't going to help me. I had to escape on my own.

But how?

I beat my fists against the glass.

No. No way I could break it with my hands.

Maybe if I lowered my shoulder and rammed the glass with it.

No way I could get any speed. I was knee-deep in scorpions.

Maybe if I dropped onto my back and *kicked* the glass?

No. I couldn't kick it hard enough to break it.

Scorpions wrapped around my waist. A pincer reached up and snapped at my neck. Missed me by an inch!

How could I escape? How?

Suddenly, I had an idea.

A frantic, desperate idea. My only chance.

# 15

I batted away a snapping scorpion. I struggled to my knees. Then I gathered up all my strength, reached both hands up, and jumped as high as I could. I grabbed the top of the case.

It was seven feet tall. Above my head. No way I could climb out.

But I pulled my head up above the edge. And I shouted to the Purple Rage: "You GEEK! You CREAMPUFF! You WIMP!"

He went on talking into the camera. He thumped his chest and talked about how angry he was.

"YOU DUMB CREEP!" I shouted. "You FAT WIMP!"

That got his attention.

He turned to me. "What did you say?"

"You BABY! You WORM!" I screamed. "You're no match for the incredible Dr. Maniac!"

He stomped up to the case. His eyes flamed red and his face turned deep purple. "Know what

CRUNCHES my CREDENZA?" he boomed. "YOU do! How DARE you!"

"You're PITIFUL!" I cried, hoisting myself up to the top of the case. "You're DIRT! You're ROADKILL!"

His eyes bulged. His mouth flew open. His nostrils flared, and his teeth began to chatter.

I waited for his head to explode!

Instead, he let out a roar. "Face the power of my *Breath of Fury*!" he boomed.

The Purple Rage sucked in a deep breath, so deep his chest popped out like a beach ball. And then he blew his Breath of Fury — a hurricane-force wind — at the case.

The glass shattered and shards crashed and clattered in all directions.

Scorpions went sailing out of the cage and flew to the wall, flailing their pincers.

The force of his breath made me do a backward somersault. I toppled out of the cage, onto the floor. It took me a few seconds to gain my balance. Then I spun to my feet.

My escape plan had worked. I was out of the case. But now I *really* had to escape!

Snarling like an angry dog, the Purple Rage dove for me.

With a cry, I grabbed two scorpions. I heaved them at him — and took off running.

He let out a roar. I felt his Breath of Fury on my

back. It pushed me out the door, into a long underground hallway.

The hall was lined on both sides by big color photos of the Purple Rage. As I ran past them, his face stared out angrily in picture after picture.

I heard his thudding footsteps behind me. Catching up fast.

"This really GRIPES my GOATEE!" he bellowed. "Come back, kid. I'm only trying to HELP you!"

*Help me? Help me feed his scorpions?*

I reached the door at the end of the hall. Twisted the knob. And shoved it open.

It led into a wide dressing room. As I ran through it, I saw open closets on both sides. Hanging in the closets dangled pair after pair of purple tights and bodysuits.

A small closet at the end was piled high with purple boots.

The Rage thundered after me. I grabbed a handful of boots and tossed them into his path.

He stomped over them and kept coming, screaming and snarling.

I found another hallway and ran faster. A dark wooden door stood at the end of the hall.

Gasping for breath, I flung the door open — and stepped through.

My feet kicked air. Nothing beneath them. No floor. No ground!

"WHOOOA!" I let out a startled cry. My hands flew above my head as I dropped straight down.

I dropped hard into a deep darkness.

And landed with a *SPLASH*.

Icy water rose over me. I held my breath as I sank into it.

A sewer. It didn't take long to figure out I had dropped into a deep, fast-flowing sewer.

The sewer water was thick and lumpy. Like cold pea soup.

I thrashed my arms and legs and struggled to stay afloat. My hands splashed against chunks of rotten garbage.

"Ohhhhhh." It smelled like week-old vomit. I started to choke and gag.

I reached for the sewer wall with both hands. But the current swept me up and pulled me away.

Was that a dead rat floating beside me?

No. Only a rat's *head*.

My stomach lurched.

The current pulled harder, carrying me into darkness. I crashed against the sewer wall. Bounced off. Tried to kick away.

Crashed again.

The putrid, disgusting water splashed over my head. I felt myself sink under the surface. I tried to pull myself up. But panic froze my body. I couldn't think. Couldn't move.

My chest throbbed. Couldn't breathe . . . drowning . . . *I'm going to drown*, I realized. *Drown in this putrid, swirling gunk.*

# 16

Finally, I got my legs moving. I kicked hard and rose to the surface, sputtering and gasping.

Shaking the thick gloppy sewage from my eyes, I spotted something up ahead — something jutting from the sewer wall. A ladder?

Yes. A ladder. I could see it glowing in a beam of yellow sunlight.

A way out!

I held my breath as the current carried me closer . . . closer. I made a desperate grab for it.

Missed.

Grabbed again. This time I caught the second rung. Holding on with both hands, I pulled my body up from the water. "Yes! Yes!" My cries were hoarse and weak.

My shoes slid off the slimy metal rungs. I held on with both hands. Gasping for breath, I lifted myself out, rung by rung.

It seemed to take forever. My body felt like it weighed a thousand pounds!

Finally, I reached the top. I hoisted myself through a sewer grate and onto the street. I pressed my hands on my knees and struggled to catch my breath.

Water rolled off me. My wet T-shirt clung to my skin. I pulled a pukey brown blob of goo out of my tangled, matted hair.

I smelled as if I'd been sprayed by a hundred skunks. Wiping sewage off my face, I pushed my hair back and gazed around. The street sign on the corner read WAYNE STREET.

"Hey!" I uttered a cry. I was only two blocks from home!

I didn't have the strength to run. So I half walked, half dragged myself across the front lawns all the way to my house.

As I trudged up the driveway, I thought about Brooke. *She probably escaped those security guards*, I decided. *She's probably safe at home by now.*

The front door swung open as I limped up the front walk. Mom stepped out, her dark eyes wide with surprise.

"Robby!" she cried. "Where *were* you?"

She studied me up and down. Then she pressed her hands against her cheeks. "Oh, my!" she murmured. "Have you been *swimming*?"

"No," I choked out. "It's a long story. I —"

"Robby, you stink to high heaven!" she cried. "Why did you run away? What on earth have you been *doing*?"

I wanted to tell her everything. But she didn't give me a chance.

She grabbed me by my hair and tugged me into the house. "Go upstairs," she ordered. "Take off those disgusting wet clothes. Take a shower. No. Take *two* showers. You *reek*! I've never smelled anything so bad in all my life."

"I — I can explain," I choked out. "Mom, some very weird stuff happened to me today."

"Not now," she said. "Go take a shower first. I can't believe you wandered off, with your brother Sam missing."

"But —"

The phone rang.

Mom hurried across the room to answer it. She began talking softly. After a few seconds, she turned pale. Her shoulders slumped. She shook her head.

"Mom — what is it?" I asked, hurrying over to her. "What's wrong?"

She set down the phone. "I don't believe it," she murmured.

"What?" I cried. "What happened?"

"That was Brooke's mom," she said. "Brooke is missing, too."

# 17

I spent a long time in the shower. I soaped myself again and again. I wondered if I could *ever* wash the smell off my skin.

The shower gave me time to think about Brooke.

She came with me to the TV station. She followed me in that wild chase up the stairs to the roof. But she never made it to the roof.

Did the TV security guys grab her? If they did, they wouldn't keep her for long.

So where *was* she?

Should I go back to the TV station and search for her?

I dried myself off. I smelled my arm. No trace of sewer rot.

Thinking about Sam and Brooke, I walked into my room and began pulling on jeans and a clean T-shirt.

Did the Purple Rage take Brooke away?

No. No way. She never stepped onto the roof. The Rage never saw Brooke.

I shook out my wet hair, then brushed it back with both hands.

As I passed my desk, I saw that my laptop was on. I squinted at the screen.

What was that? Something I'd never seen before?

I leaned on the desk and lowered my gaze to the screen.

"Huh?" A gasp escaped my throat.

I stared at a comic strip in bold colors. I recognized the character.

Dr. Maniac.

Drawn in my style. But *new*.

A new Dr. Maniac comic.

My mouth dropped open in shock as I started to read it.

"What's *up* with this?" I cried. "How can there be a new strip? I didn't draw this one!"

# 18

The strip showed Dr. Maniac standing on a city street. His leopard-skin cape fell behind his shoulders. He raised a gloved fist at the reader.

"I'm going to kidnap every kid in the city!" he bragged in the dialogue balloon above his head. "Every kid in the city, one by one. And I'm going to make them ice-skate twenty-four hours a day! It'll be the biggest *ice show* in history!"

In the next panel, Dr. Maniac had an evil grin on his face. "Do you know how much money that will bring me?" he asked.

"You're crazy!" said a character beside him.

"I'm not crazy — I'm a MANIAC!" the evil supervillain boomed. "And my giant ice show — all singing, all skating — is going to make me the RICHEST maniac on earth!"

I scrolled down to see the rest of the comic strip. In the next panel, Dr. Maniac bellowed: "I'll call it *MANIAC ON ICE!* I love it! I LOVE show business! Hahahahaha!"

Then he pulled two kids into view. Leaning onto my desk, staring into the glow of the laptop screen, I cried out in disbelief.

Sam and Brooke!

He grabbed each one of them under an arm and took off. He flew them to a large brick building at the edge of town.

The building looked familiar. I knew I'd seen it before.

A sign on one wall read: PUBLIC SWIMMING POOL. DANGER — NO LIFEGUARD ON DUTY.

My heart pounded as I kept reading.

Dr. Maniac carried Sam and Brooke to the indoor pool and dropped them on the side. They were surrounded by yellow-tiled walls. No one else there.

I stared at the pool. The water had been frozen. It was solid ice, a skating rink.

Dr. Maniac handed ice skates to Sam and Brooke. "Lace them up tight," he ordered. "Start skating back and forth."

"For how long?" Sam asked.

"For as long as your NOSE!" Dr. Maniac exclaimed. Then he tossed his head back and laughed his hyena laugh.

"That doesn't make any sense. You're crazy!" Brooke cried.

"As CRAZY as a monkey in a meatball factory!" he screamed. "Hahahahaha! I've got a MILLION of 'em!"

Sam and Brooke laced up their skates. They had no choice. Then Dr. Maniac pushed them onto the ice. They started skating the length of the long swimming pool, back and forth.

Dr. Maniac grinned again. "That will keep you two busy!" he said. "Twenty-four hours a day! The audiences will LOVE it! Now I'm going to add all the other kids in town to our skating troupe! What a good show! Hahahahahaha!"

Leaning forward, Sam and Brooke skated side by side. They kept casting frightened glances at each other. They both looked terrified.

I tried to scroll down to see more. But that's where the comic strip ended.

For a long time, I stood there staring at the screen. My mind was doing flip-flops. I couldn't believe what I'd just seen.

How could there be a new *Dr. Maniac* strip that I didn't draw?

Did the characters I created really come to life? Sam and Brooke really disappeared. What was real and what was just a comic strip?

I suddenly felt dizzy. This was too hard to figure out. My head started to ache.

I ran to the head of the stairs. "Mom!" I shouted. "Come upstairs. Hurry! I want to show you something."

A few seconds later, Mom started up the stairs. Behind her, I saw the policeman who had been here earlier — Officer Rawls.

69

He reached the top of the stairs and stared at me coldly. "Robby, you're in serious trouble," he said softly.

Mom started to say something. But Rawls raised his hand to silence her.

Then he turned back to me. "Your brother and your friend have both disappeared," he said. "Why did you run away this afternoon? I think you know a *lot more* than you're letting on."

He stuck his face up close to mine. "Robby," he said, "you'd better start talking. Now."

I stepped back. "I didn't run away," I said. "I —"

"Robby, you have to tell us everything you know," Mom interrupted. "Do you know where Sam and Brooke are? *Do* you?"

"It's all in the comic strip," I said.

"Kid, we don't have time for comics now," Officer Rawls said. "Tell us —"

"Come look at this," I said. I spun away from them and started jogging to my room. "This will explain everything. It's a comic strip that I didn't draw. It — it just appeared on my computer!"

They followed me into my room. I pointed at the laptop screen. "Sam and Brooke are in the strip," I said. "Look!"

They stared hard at the screen. I turned and stared, too.

The screen was blank. Solid gray.

My heart started to pound. "It was here a second ago," I said. I leaned over the laptop and began scrolling up and down.

Nothing.

A blank screen.

Officer Rawls put a hand on my shoulder. "Enough about comic strips," he said. "Do you want to tell us what's really going on?"

"I — don't know," I stammered. "Really."

"Do you have any idea where the two missing kids might be?" Rawls asked.

"In the comic strip, Dr. Maniac took them to that abandoned swimming pool across town," I said. "He froze the pool and turned it into an ice rink. He plans to kidnap all the kids in town and make them skate in his ice show."

Officer Rawls let out a long sigh. "This isn't a comic book, kid," he growled. "You're starting to annoy me. Do you think this is some kind of a joke?"

He didn't wait for my answer. He turned and lumbered down the hall and down the stairs. Mom gave me a worried glance. Then she followed him downstairs.

I could hear them arguing. "Your son is totally mental," I heard the officer say. "Comic books have gone to his brain."

I heard the front door slam. Out my bedroom window, I saw Officer Rawls stomp across our front yard. He climbed into his patrol car and sped off.

*Am I a total wacko?* I asked myself. *I don't think so.*

I waited till Mom and Dad went out. Then I left the house.

The afternoon sun was falling behind the trees. I leaned into the cool breeze as I made my way to the bus stop.

I knew where that abandoned swimming pool was. I took swimming lessons there when I was in preschool. Officer Rawls didn't believe me. So I had to check it out myself.

Did the comic strip tell the truth?

The bus ride took nearly half an hour. It gave me a lot of time to think about my crazy plan. Was I really following a comic character that I made up? Could it really lead me to Sam and Brooke?

I found myself in a neighborhood of run-down apartment buildings and abandoned stores. It didn't take long to find the old brick building that held the swimming pool.

I started to the front door — then stopped. Maybe Dr. Maniac was inside. It might be a lot smarter to sneak in through the back. I remembered a back door that opened onto the pool.

At the corner, a big dog was nosing around in an overturned trash can. I slipped past him and made my way to the alley in back.

The building blocked out the sunlight. I walked carefully through the darkness. I grabbed the knob and tried the back door. To my surprise, it pulled open easily. Light poured out onto the alley.

I opened the door just a crack and peeked inside.

The bright glare of the white ice made me blink. Yes. The frozen pool. Just like in the strip.

I pulled the door open a little wider. Then I took a deep breath and crept inside.

A blast of icy air greeted me. My eyes still hadn't adjusted to the glare. The yellow-tiled walls glowed like sunlight.

I gazed at the giant ice rink. "Hey!" I let out a shout when I saw the two kids.

Yes! A boy and a girl, skating together. Leaning forward. Skating away from me.

"Hey!" I leaped onto the ice and began running after them. "Sam! Brooke! It's me!" I cried.

They didn't turn around.

Dr. Maniac suddenly appeared on the ice just ahead of me. I uttered a startled gasp. He was shorter than I'd drawn him. And his belly bulged inside his tight costume.

I tried to stop — and slid for four or five feet. "NOOOO!" I shouted as I lost my balance and fell. I landed hard on my knees and elbows on the frozen surface.

Before I could scramble to my feet, a heavy net fell over me.

It sent me sprawling onto my stomach. My face hit, and I got a mouthful of ice.

I struggled onto my back. I tried to kick and thrash free. But the heavy net held me down.

Sweeping his cape behind him, Dr. Maniac stood over me. He grinned down at me. "Join our show, Robby!" he exclaimed. "The more the merrier!"

"Let me GO!" I screamed. "And them, too!"

I raised my head as Sam and Brooke skated up to me.

Whoa. Wait. Not Sam and Brooke.

Two kids I'd never seen before.

I shoved the net with both hands and sat up. Behind the two kids, I saw a young woman gliding toward us over the ice. She had red hair and sparkling blue eyes.

She wore a bright red mask, a very short red skirt over red tights, and a red top. And a red cape that flowed down to her shiny red boots.

"The Scarlet Starlet!" Dr. Maniac cried. "Glad you could join us!"

"Where are the spotlights?" The Scarlet Starlet demanded. "Where are the cameras? Where are my adoring fans?"

"I'm trying to keep it quiet," Dr. Maniac replied. "Until I fill my ice rink with kids."

She tossed back her long red hair. "But I need a lot of attention," she said. "Don't forget — I'm the Scarlet Starlet!"

"Don't worry," Dr. Maniac said. "When our twenty-four-hour ice show begins, you'll get LOTS of attention! More attention than a hamster in an encyclopedia factory! Hahahaha!"

That didn't make any *sense* to me. But it made her smile. She slapped him a high five. Her long fingernails were also bright red.

Still smiling, she lowered her gaze to me. "Maniac," she said, "I see we have a new skater!"

"Please call me DOCTOR Maniac," he scolded. "I have a college degree in Maniacal Studies."

"Well, who is our new skater?" she asked.

"I'm NOT going to skate!" I cried. I pushed at the net with all my strength. "Let me out of here! You two can't get away with this!"

Dr. Maniac and the Scarlet Starlet both laughed. "He's a funny one," the Scarlet Starlet said.

"What have you done with my brother?" I screamed. "Where is my friend Brooke?"

The Scarlet Starlet's red smile faded. She leaned down close to me. Behind her mask, her eyes turned to ice. "Just forget about them," she said. "You'll never see them again."

# 20

*Never see them again?*

Her words sent a chill down my back.

"I — don't understand," I stammered. "Where are they? What have you done with them?"

The two supervillains didn't answer. They each took an end of the heavy net and lifted it high.

I scrambled out from under it. I tried to run. I had to get away from them. I had to get help. Maybe Officer Rawls would believe me now.

I took four or five running steps. Then my sneakers slid out from under me. And I fell facedown on the ice again.

Dr. Maniac moved quickly to pick me up. He brushed ice off the front of my T-shirt.

"Don't worry. I have skates in your size," he said. "You can join the show." He pulled a pair of skates from a large box and handed them to me. "Start skating twenty-four hours. You'll get used to it. Good exercise!"

"I'm not going to skate," I said. "Not until you tell me where Sam and Brooke are."

Dr. Maniac's face twisted in anger. "If you don't skate," he said, "I'll tickle you till you puke!"

"You're CRAZY!" I cried.

"I'm not crazy — I'm a MANIAC!" he screamed.

The Scarlet Starlet patted my head. "Better put on the skates," she said softly. "I've *watched* him tickle people. It isn't pretty."

I gazed over her scarlet shoulders to the door. Could I dart past them and make it out of there before they grabbed me?

The other two kids had started skating back and forth again. *No way* I wanted to join them. I knew once I started, they'd never let me stop.

Then I saw a blur of purple at the other end of the ice rink. The two supervillains saw it, too. We stared as the blur grew larger.

I blinked in disbelief — as the Purple Rage came sliding over the ice to us, both fists raised.

"Know what really BITES my GIRAFFE?" he boomed. "Having to rescue kids and battle you two skunks again!" He let out an angry roar.

"Yaaaay!" I cheered. But then I heard Dr. Maniac whisper to the Scarlet Starlet. "Don't worry. I know how to handle this red-faced rooster."

"Let these kids go!" the Purple Rage shouted.

Dr. Maniac put his hands at his bulging waist, tossed back his head — and *laughed*.

The Scarlet Starlet copied him. She opened her red lips wide and laughed, too.

The Rage's face grew redder. His eyes nearly popped out of his head.

"Maybe you didn't hear me!" he screamed. "I said, let these kids go! Or you will face the *rage* of the Purple Rage!"

Dr. Maniac shook his head and giggled. The Scarlet Starlet hee-hawed, slapping her knees.

The Rage's face was bright purple now. His cheeks puffed out. His nostrils flared. His chest heaved as he struggled to breathe. "Feel my RAAAAAAGE!" he boomed.

The two villains laughed and giggled. They laughed so hard, their faces were wet with tears.

The Purple Rage shot both fists high above his head. His chest ballooned out. His eyes bulged. He let out a furious roar.

And he EXPLODED. Just like that. POP.

And he burst apart into a million icky pieces.

The pieces flew all over the ice.

Dr. Maniac grinned at the Scarlet Starlet. "I told you I knew how to handle him. Easy as sitting on a lemon meringue pie! Just make him really, really, really angry — and he'll bust! Hahahahaha!"

He shoved the skates back into my hands. "Okay," he said. "We don't have to worry about him anymore. Start skating."

# 21

I pulled on the skates and started to slide back and forth across the big rink with the other two kids. I had no choice.

I had a million questions I wanted to ask. But the three of us didn't talk. Too scared, I guess. The only sound was the scrape of our skates on the hard surface.

I couldn't stop thinking about Sam and Brooke.

If Dr. Maniac had grabbed them both, why weren't they here skating with us? Why did the Scarlet Starlet say they were gone for good?

*Just forget about them. You'll never see them again.*

Every time I heard those words in my mind, my stomach tightened. My legs became weak. I felt sick.

There were big blobby pieces of the Purple Rage all over the ice. We had to skate carefully around them.

It was totally gross. If only he could have controlled his anger . . .

I let out sigh after sigh. Was he our last hope?

How long did I skate? Maybe an hour. Maybe two hours.

More kids joined us. The two supervillains were keeping their promise. They were busy grabbing all the kids in town.

Soon, the skating rink was mobbed. It was a horrifying sight. Dozens and dozens of sad-looking kids, skating . . . skating silently . . . all too terrified to stop.

Sweat poured down my face. My long hair was soaked. My legs trembled with every move.

I pushed my way through the crowd, skating slowly, painfully. I felt exhausted. I knew I couldn't skate much longer.

"Sam? Brooke? Where are you?" I muttered to myself.

How could I get out of there? How could I find them?

Finally, I began to think clearly. There were at least two hundred kids trapped there. And there were only two supervillains.

We had them totally outnumbered.

If we all stampeded for the exit, some of us might get stopped. But a lot of us would escape. And we could get help for the others.

I raised my eyes to the back wall. A huge video screen hung high on the wall. On the screen, the

Scarlet Starlet and Dr. Maniac gazed down at us. Their eyes sparkled happily as they watched us skate.

*Maybe I can wipe those smiles off their faces,* I thought.

An enormous round clock — black numbers against white — hung next to the video screen. The clock said eight-twenty.

I lowered my hands to my knees and began gliding through the skaters. "At eight-thirty, head for the door," I whispered. "Pass it on."

I crisscrossed the rink, trying to reach as many kids as I could. "Eight-thirty, we escape," I whispered again and again. "Head for the door. Pass it on."

Kids gazed up at the big video screen with frightened looks on their faces.

"Keep skating. Keep skating," I whispered. "Pass it on. At eight-thirty, we head for the door."

My legs ached. My heart pounded in my chest. My skates scraped the ice as I kept my eyes on the clock.

One minute to go. I could feel the excitement build among all of us trapped kids. A hush fell over the rink.

I tensed my leg muscles and prepared to burst to the exit.

The seconds ticked away.

At first, I thought the *cracking* sound was coming from outside.

But then I heard kids scream. I saw a girl slide onto her back. Her feet shot straight up into the air.

The *cracking* grew louder.

I slid to a stop as chunks of ice sank in front of me.

"It's MELTING!" a boy screamed. "It's all MELTING!"

# 22

A deafening roar rang out. The ice cracked and fell away.

All around me, kids were sinking into deep, bone-chilling water. Screams and startled cries echoed off the tile walls.

I raised my eyes to the video screen. Dr. Maniac stood at a computer, typing frantically as the Scarlet Starlet looked on.

He was melting the ice.

He had it all set up. He knew exactly how to block our escape.

The surface cracked beneath me. I let out a groan as I went plunging down.

The icy water rose up over my knees. Shuddering and shivering, I thrashed my arms helplessly. I sank to my waist and kept dropping.

The water was so cold, I could feel my whole body going numb.

All around me, kids shouted and cried and

splashed and kicked. Kids tried to swim out of it, but chunks of ice blocked their way.

"G-gotta move," I muttered to myself, shivering and shaking. "B-before I'm totally numb."

Too cold to swim. Too deep to walk.

I hurtled forward . . . pulled myself . . . used every bit of strength I had. Finally, shivering, my teeth chattering, I crawled from the freezing pool.

Dr. Maniac stood nearby at the computer controls. Could I get to him before he saw me?

With a shudder, I climbed to my feet — staggered toward him, water running off me. Lurched ahead, shivering and shaking — and *dove* at Dr. Maniac.

I didn't think. My brain was totally frozen.

I had no plan. I just threw myself at him.

With a groan, I grabbed him around the waist. He struggled. Tried to spin out of my grasp.

But I held on. Held on tight. Gasping for breath, I pulled myself up on him.

I grabbed at his cape. My wet hands slid off.

He started to duck away.

I raised both hands — and grabbed his face.

"Yes!" I uttered. My whole body shuddered and shivered.

I tightened my fingers around his face — *and it came off!*

His face came off in my hands. It was a MASK!

I tossed the mask down and stared into his *real* face. And screamed at the top of my lungs: "SAM! It's YOU!"

# 23

Shivering from the freezing water that soaked my clothes, I stared at my brother. "Sam?"

He grabbed the mask from me. "I'm not your brother anymore," he said. "I'm Dr. Maniac."

"But — how?" I choked out.

The Scarlet Starlet stepped between us. "Don't ask questions," she snapped. She lifted her mask so I could see her real face.

"Brooke!" I gasped. "You, too?"

"I told you to forget about us," she said. "Sam and Brooke are gone forever." She pulled the scarlet mask back over her face.

My mind was spinning. I felt dizzy.

Meanwhile, kids were screaming and crying. I turned and saw terrified faces, thrashing arms and legs. Kids were swimming and splashing, trying frantically to get out of the ice-clogged pool.

On the big video screen on the back wall, I glimpsed myself standing between Sam and

Brooke. I could see the totally shocked expression on my face.

I grabbed my brother by the shoulders. "But why, Sam?" I asked. "Why did you choose to be evil?"

Sam's dark eyes locked on mine. "You said it first, Robby," he replied. "You said the villains are always more interesting."

He pulled the mask down over his head. "I'm a maniac now. I'm not your pudgy kid brother anymore."

"But, Sam —" I protested.

"You were always the talented one," he said, sneering. "Mr. Talented Artist with his awesome comic strips. And I was just the chubby joke. Well . . . not anymore. I'm *evil*, Robby — and soon I'm going to be RICH!"

"No, this is wrong!" I cried. "This is totally WRONG! Sam, you have to come home!"

He and Brooke stepped close and sandwiched me between them. "Are you with us or against us?" Brooke said.

"With us or against us?" Sam demanded. It wasn't a question. It was a *threat*.

They pressed against me. I could *feel* their evil.

"With us or against us?" Sam demanded.

I couldn't believe it. I felt terrified. Terrified of my own brother and my friend.

They glared at me, waiting for my answer.

I took a deep breath. "AGAINST you," I said finally. "*Now* what are you going to do?"

# 24

Before they could answer, the back doors crashed open. All three of us turned and saw a group of black-uniformed police officers swarm into the rink.

"NOOOO!" Dr. Maniac let out an angry cry.

The Scarlet Starlet gasped and took a step back. She tripped over her cape and nearly fell over.

At least a dozen cops ran in. Some waded into the pool and began pulling out the freezing, frightened kids. Others came running to the front of the pool.

I recognized Officer Rawls. He led five or six other cops toward us. "Good work, Robby!" he shouted. "You led us right to them!"

Dr. Maniac and the Scarlet Starlet were too stunned to move. The cops surrounded us.

"You two villains are going away for a long time!" Rawls shouted.

Dr. Maniac tossed back his head and laughed. "You loser cops will never take us!" he cried.

The cops made a grab for them.

I heard a soft *pop*. And Dr. Maniac and the Scarlet Starlet vanished.

The cops grabbed at the air.

"Where did they go?" Rawls cried. "Don't let them get away!"

I pointed to the huge video screen at the back wall. "There they are!" I shouted.

Yes. The two villains stared down at us from the big screen. "The world will NEVER be safe from us!" the Scarlet Starlet shouted.

Dr. Maniac laughed his hyena laugh again. "She's right!" he declared. "When she's right, she's right! She's as right as a mongoose at a picnic! You are all DOOMED!"

I glanced at the computer near the wall. And suddenly, I had an idea.

A frightening idea. But an idea that just might work.

I moved to the computer keyboard. I hesitated. I didn't want to do it. I really didn't.

But I knew I had no choice.

I raised my finger to the keyboard. And I pressed the DELETE key.

And with another *pop*, Dr. Maniac and the Scarlet Starlet vanished from the video screen — vanished for good.

# 25

Mom and I were in my bedroom. Mom leaned over me with her hands on my shoulders, reading the comic strip on my laptop.

It was a long story, the longest I had ever drawn. I called it *Dr. Maniac vs. Robby Schwartz*.

Mom finally finished it and took a step back. "Wow," she said. "That's excellent, Robby. Very exciting. The swimming pool scene is terrific."

"Did you really like it?" I asked.

"Yes," she said. "But it has such a sad ending. You deleted your brother and your friend Brooke?"

I nodded. "I thought it was a perfect ending," I said. "Good triumphed over evil. But it was also sad."

"I like the way you mixed the real world with the pretend world," Mom said. "Very clever. I know you *hate* being an only child. So you invented a brother and sister for yourself."

"Yeah, I guess that's why I made up Sam and Taylor," I said.

Mom patted my shoulder. "Maybe you spend so much time at your computer because you're lonely," she said.

"I'm not lonely, Mom," I replied. "I just like to make up stories."

"Well, that's good," Mom said.

"I'm going to write a new comic with all new characters," I told her. "Maybe I'll give myself *three* brothers and *three* sisters!"

That made Mom laugh. The phone rang. She gave me a wave and hurried downstairs.

I turned back to my laptop.

"Whoa!" I let out a startled cry. There was a drawing on the screen I'd never seen before.

In the drawing, Dr. Maniac and the Scarlet Starlet stood side by side. And standing next to them was my imaginary sister, Taylor.

"Hey — I didn't draw this!" I cried. I leaned close and studied the screen. They were standing in an amusement park.

"I . . . don't believe this!" I muttered. "How is this *possible*?"

Then dialogue balloons popped up over their heads.

Taylor said: "Listen, Robby, next time, I want a BIGGER part! I didn't get to do ANYTHING in your dumb story!"

The Scarlet Starlet said: "We don't like your ending. We have a BETTER ending!"

And finally, Dr. Maniac, grinning out at me like an evil fiend, said: "You won't like *our* ending, Robby. But we'll be showing it to you — *real soon*! We'll be WAITING for you — in HorrorLand!"

# ENTER
# HORRORLAND

# THE STORY SO FAR...

Several kids received mysterious invitations to be special guests at HorrorLand theme park. They were supposed to have a week of scary fun — but the scares quickly became **TOO REAL**.

Britney Crosby and Molly Molloy disappeared. Billy Deep was horrified when his sister, Sheena, became invisible. Then Sheena disappeared, too.

A park guide — a Horror named Byron — warned the kids they were all in danger. Byron tried to help them. But then he was dragged away by other Horrors.

Why are they all in danger? The kids are desperate to find Byron to get some answers.

Carly Beth Caldwell and her friend Sabrina Mason arrived at HorrorLand a few days after the others. They quickly got themselves lost and locked into an area of the park called Wolfsbane Forest.

Who else is trapped in this forest of werewolves? You guessed it — Robby Schwartz.

Robby continues the story. . . .

Wolfsbane Forest. When I saw the big sign at the entrance, I thought it sounded like a place in one of my comic stories.

But it was real. *Too real!*

A forest where wolves and werewolves walked free. They howled at the moon and padded on their furry paws over the crackling dead leaves on the forest floor.

I could see the glowing eyes of the inhuman beasts through the dark trees. Were they stalking me? Stalking their *prey*?

A chill shook my body, as if someone had dropped ice down my back.

HorrorLand is an amusement park, right? And Wolfsbane Forest is one of its biggest attractions. It's *supposed* to be fun.

I told myself the half-man, half-wolf creatures were machines. Big toys run by someone in a hidden control room.

But they looked so real, so menacing. Even in bright daylight, I stayed on the alert and kept my distance.

But now it was night. And I listened to the hungry howls all around me. And each sound made me jump with fright.

How did I let this happen?

Why did I stay so long in Werewolf Village?

It was my first day at HorrorLand. Yes, I was excited. When the invitation came in the mail, I forgot about everything else. I HAD to go!

I mean, I know I got that weird message from Dr. Maniac and everything, but would *you* give up a free week as a special guest at the coolest theme park ever?

Why was Werewolf Village the first place I visited? I draw so many comics that take place in woods and forests. I love imagining the scary beasts and monsters that live in the forest. I couldn't wait to see what the HorrorLand people created in their forest.

But I lost track of the time.

Under the thick trees of the forest, I didn't even see the sun go down. And now, I stumbled through the dark, searching for the way out. Listening to the angry growls and long, mournful wolf howls.

It gave me lots of ideas for my next strip: *Dr. Maniac vs. the White Werewolf.*

Or maybe, *Dr. Maniac vs. Wonder Werewolf*!

Who would win that battle? How would the evil Maniac defeat an immortal Wolf Man?

I was thinking hard about these questions. I didn't see the jagged rock in front of me. I let out a cry as I stumbled over it. My arms shot out to stop my fall.

*I landed on somebody!*

High, shrill screams made my heart stop beating.

My arms were tangled in somebody's arms. We bumped heads.

I struggled to pull away. The screams rang in my ears.

Staggering back, I saw two girls about my age. Even in the dark, I could see that their eyes were wide with fear. Huddled together, they backed away from me.

Breathing hard, I brushed off the front of my jeans. "Uh . . . hi," I said. "Guess I scared you, huh?"

"What are you *doing* here?" the taller one cried.

"Your hair — it's so . . . wild! And it's so dark here. We . . . we thought you were a *werewolf*!" her friend said.

"No. I don't even shave yet," I told her.

Always keep it light — right?

They still stared at me like I was some kind of hideous creature. *Robby Schwartz, Terror of the Forest!*

101

"Sorry I scared you," I said. "I tripped over something. I can't find my way out of this place."

The two girls told me their names — Carly Beth and Sabrina.

"I'm Robby Schwartz," I said. "I've been wandering around in circles for hours. I never was a Boy Scout. I don't know how to read a compass."

Carly Beth frowned. "I don't think a compass would help," she said.

She pointed to a tall wire gate. "Sabrina and I got lost, too. We saw some horrible men in cages. Some of them had wolf snouts. It wasn't fun. It looked real. Finally, we found this gate."

Sabrina walked to the gate and tugged at the metal lock. "We're locked in. But there has to be an unlocked gate somewhere — right?"

"Unless they lock up the whole forest for the night," I said.

Carly Beth hugged herself. "There *has* to be a way out. Otherwise, kids would get trapped in here every night."

"Maybe that's how they feed the wolves," I said.

It was supposed to be a joke.

But no one laughed. Out of the silence, we heard rapid footsteps. We froze — and listened to the thud of heavy paws on the ground. Low snarls . . . growling wolves . . . hungry growls . . . wolves moving fast through the forest.

"They . . . they're coming for us," I whispered.

# 2

They burst out from the trees. Four of them. Heads lowered. Eyes glowing like yellow marbles.

My mouth dropped open. I froze in fear.

I knew I looked like a terrified character in one of my comics. And suddenly, a scene from one of my first stories flashed through my mind.

*Dr. Maniac vs. the Mighty Mole Boy.*

I didn't think about it. My body just moved. I dropped to my knees on the soft ground in front of the gate. And I began pawing at the dirt.

I dug frantically. Luckily, the dirt was soft as sand. I scooped up handfuls of dirt under the fence and shoved them aside. Pawing like the Mole Creature in my comic strip.

The growling wolves formed a line behind us. One of them lifted its head to the moon, as if signaling for an attack.

Breathing hard, I shoveled an opening big enough to slide my hands in. I pushed my hands into the shallow hole and dropped onto my stomach. Then I kicked with both feet. Kicked hard and fast . . . again . . . again.

The bottom of the fence scraped my back. But I pushed myself under it and over to the other side.

Then, wiping dirt off my forehead, I turned to help the two girls. I didn't have to tell them what to do.

Sabrina was already on her stomach. She stuck both hands under the bottom of the fence. I grabbed them and started to pull her through to my side. "Duck your head! Duck your head!" I screamed.

Her hair got stuck on a wire. She let out a cry and lowered her face to the dirt. And I tugged her the rest of the way.

I turned to help Carly Beth. Behind her, I watched the wolves. Their silvery fur glistened in the moonlight. They raised their heads and let out hungry howls. They arched their backs, preparing to attack.

"Hurry, Carly Beth!" Sabrina screamed.

I grabbed Carly Beth's hands and pulled.

Her body slid heavily over the dirt. She was halfway through when the wolves attacked.

All four of them leaped at once.

She screamed so loud, I dropped her hands.

My heart pounding, I grabbed for them again. I pulled hard. But Carly Beth was stuck.

"It's got me!" Carly Beth wailed. "OWWWW! It's got my FOOT!"

"*Noooo!*" A hoarse cry burst from my throat.

I pictured Carly Beth's foot chewed to pieces.

But no. "Carly Beth — the wolf doesn't have your foot!" I choked out. "Your foot is caught in the fence."

She gave a hard kick. Her shoe caught in the fence. But I pulled her the rest of the way to my side.

The ferocious wolves leaped — and crashed into the fence. Howling angrily, they leaped again. Too late.

Carly Beth jumped to her feet, struggling to catch her breath. "Th-they're real!" she stammered.

The wolves stared at us, their heads lowered. Like a staring contest. They didn't move or blink.

"Let's get away from here," Sabrina said. She tugged her friend back from the fence. "At least we got out of the forest. Let's go back to the hotel."

Carly Beth turned to me. "You saved us from those wolves," she said. "Digging under the fence like that."

"That's me. Robby Schwartz, superhero," I said. "Know where I can buy a cape and tights?"

"We've got to find the other kids," Carly Beth said. "We've got to tell them what Sabrina and I heard today. And what's going on."

She pulled her shoe out from under the fence. Then, taking long strides, she and Sabrina followed the path toward the Stagger Inn, our hotel. I had to jog to catch up to them.

"Other kids? What do you mean?" I asked, stepping between them.

"We met these kids," Carly Beth said. "Other special guests. They said scary things happened to them here in the park. They said a Horror named Byron warned them."

"Warned them about *what*?" I said.

"Warned them that we're all in danger," Carly Beth replied.

Danger? Suddenly, I remembered the end of that comic strip. Dr. Maniac warning me he'd be waiting at HorrorLand. Maybe I should have listened. . . .

We passed the Crocodile Café. A neon sign over the door read: GRAB A BITE. GOOD FOOD IN A SNAP! I

106

could see Black Lagoon Water Park in the distance.

The park was still crowded with kids and families. It cheered me up to be back in a crowd. We were out of that frightening Werewolf Village. Why did Carly Beth still look so totally terrified?

"I didn't believe those kids when they told me about the missing girls," Carly Beth said. "They said two girls — Britney and Molly — totally disappeared. And a girl named Sheena turned invisible," she said. "I thought maybe they were trying to scare Sabrina and me."

Carly Beth shook her head. "But I believe them now."

"We heard these two Horrors talking," Sabrina said. "Marcus and Bubba. Those were their names. They didn't know Carly Beth and I could hear them."

We ducked around a Frozen Eyeballs cart. Behind the cart, a Horror in a yellow apron was piling eyeballs on a sugar cone. Painted on the side of the cart were the words: EYE SCREAM. LICK AN EYEBALL FOR LUNCH!

"What did the two Horrors say?" I asked.

"They said things were going to get a *lot* scarier for us special guests," Sabrina replied.

I squinted at her. "Seriously?"

Carly Beth frowned at me. "Don't you think

being attacked by *real wolves* was scary enough?"

"Carly Beth is right," Sabrina said. "Something frightening is going on here."

"Well . . . what should we do about it?" I asked.

Before they could answer, I felt something wrap around my ankle.

"LOOK OUT!" I screamed. My hands flew out in front of me — and I went plunging headfirst to the ground.

I hit the asphalt hard and bounced once or twice.

My breath caught in my throat. Something had brought me down. Something . . .

Why were the girls laughing?

I spun around — and saw the puffy green stuffed snake at my feet. Someone probably won it in a carnival game and dropped it.

The two girls helped pull me up. "You're an *awesome* superhero," Sabrina said.

"We won't tell anyone you tripped over a stuffed snake," Carly Beth said. "Just everyone we meet."

They both laughed again.

I held up the snake. "Look at those vicious fangs!" I said. "This snake is a *killer*. I just saved your lives *again*!"

I handed the snake to a little girl who was walking by with her parents. "You're our millionth customer!" I said. "You win a fabulous stuffed snake!"

"Thanks," she said. She flung the snake over her shoulder and kept on walking.

We watched her go. Her parents kept looking back at us.

"We've got to get serious," Carly Beth said. She started toward the hotel again. "We were almost killed back there."

"Maybe those kids found Byron, that Horror who said he wanted to help," Sabrina said.

We made our way through a group of teenagers who were playing Keep-Away with a kid's baseball cap. They tossed it back and forth, shouting and laughing.

"I just came here for fun," I told the girls. "Do you really think we were all invited for another reason?"

I didn't hear their answer. I could see them talking. But their words disappeared into the air. Something very strange was happening to me. . . .

I suddenly felt as if I were floating. As if I had left my body down on the ground, and I was hovering above it. Too far away to hear what Carly Beth and Sabrina were saying.

I struggled to concentrate on them. But I could feel myself being pulled away . . . feel my mind drifting, swimming in the air. . . .

I held my breath. Shook my head. Tried to make the strange feeling go away.

Blinking, I focused on the building up ahead. Big blue neon letters over the wide entrance announced: THE GAME PRESERVE. 100 VIDEO GAMES.

Game Preserve? A huge game arcade?

Without realizing it, I had spun away from the girls. And my legs were taking me there. My mind was already there. And I was being pulled, like by a vacuum cleaner . . . pulled to the game arcade.

"Hey — Robby!"

I heard Carly Beth shout. "Robby! Where are you going? Hey!"

"Catch you later," I said.

At least, I *think* I said it. Because my brain was already in the arcade.

And I stepped through the doors into a huge room . . . under intense blue light. The blue light washed over everything. The games looked blue . . . and the people playing them did, too. The floor and the walls glowed like blue ice.

I walked past a row of war games and then a long row of racing games, cars roaring and squealing. I saw pinball games against one wall and a wall of classic games like *Pac-Man* and *Donkey Kong*.

I didn't stop to check them out. Guns roared. Bombs exploded. Music rose and fell. I kept walking through the blue light, as if my legs knew where they were going.

I didn't have a choice.

111

Is this what it feels like to be hypnotized?

The strange blue light swirled around me like a fog. And when it finally cleared, I was standing in a tiny back room. The roars and blasts of the games behind me faded into the far distance.

I stopped — and stared in shock at the one game in the room.

A big video screen with flashing lights all around it. Evil laughter poured out of its speakers. And the title of the game filled the screen in dripping purple letters:

DR. MANIAC'S WORLD OF PAIN

I gasped. How could this be?

How could there be a Dr. Maniac game? And what was the power that pulled me here . . . that drew me to this game?

I knew I had to play it.

I moved to the counter beside the game console. A helmet with an orange visor and yellow leather gloves were waiting for me there. Next to them, I saw a stack of silver tokens.

Someone *wanted* me to play this game.

Someone got it all ready for me. But — who? And why?

And why couldn't I just turn and walk away?

I pulled the heavy helmet down over my head. I peered out through the plastic orange visor. There were speakers inside the helmet. I heard music and that deep evil laughter.

I pulled on the yellow gloves. They were light and slipped on easily.

I stepped up to the game console. I dropped a token into the slot.

It made a clicking sound. The music changed. The screen went blank.

I picked up the red-and-purple blaster gun from the side of the game machine. I tested it out a few times. It made a *zzzzzzap* sound each time I pulled the trigger.

The screen turned purple, then red. A smoky fog covered the screen. And then a figure stepped forward from out of the fog. He swirled his leopard-skin cape and floated closer.

Dr. Maniac!

My character! My creation! My *enemy*!

# 5

My hand trembled as I pushed the START button. I leaned over the console.

Could I defeat Dr. Maniac?

"I'm not crazy — I'm a MANIAC!" Dr. Maniac's voice boomed inside my helmet.

I raised the blaster, aimed it at the big M on his chest — and pulled the trigger.

I heard a drippy *bloop bloop bloop* sound.

On the video screen, Dr. Maniac tossed back his head and laughed. "You have to earn your ammo first, Robby!" he boomed. "The chase is on — loser!"

I gasped. He called me by name!

He took off and flew through a crowded city. His leopard-skin cape floated behind him as he swooped higher, then down again between tall buildings.

I aimed the blaster at the yellow feathers on his boots. Pulled the trigger.

*Bloop bloop bloop.*

Useless.

I dropped the gun and grabbed the controller. I whipped it frantically from left to right, trying to follow the flying villain. He flew through a maze of tall buildings and ducked through crowds at busy corners.

Each time I stayed with him, I racked up ammo points. The numbers rolled at the top of the screen. And I heard a sound like *powpowpow* each time I scored.

He zoomed into a subway opening, and I followed him down into the tunnel. We flew together in a wild race through the dark, twisting tunnel.

I pulled up as an ugly monster rose up on the tracks. A huge purple underground subway creature swinging a dozen deadly tentacles.

The monster filled the tunnel, blocking my path to Dr. Maniac. Yellow slime dripped off its jagged yellow teeth. Screeching at the top of its lungs, it waved its tentacles and snapped its massive jaws open to swallow me.

I jerked the controller back to stop my flight. I fumbled for the blaster. Grabbed it — and pulled the trigger.

And two words in big green letters filled the screen:

GAME OVER.

Breathing hard, I leaned both hands on the game console. The game ended just as I was racking up big ammo points.

I reached for another token. Should I play another game?

No, I decided. I've got to catch up with Carly Beth and Sabrina.

But then Dr. Maniac's grinning face appeared on the screen. "Robby, you surely know that a loser never quits, and a quitter never loses! Or *something* like that!" he screamed.

He tossed his head back and laughed. "I'm not crazy — I'm a MANIAC!"

He took off again. This time, he was flying over a crowded beach. Gold-and-green ocean waves tossed beneath him.

And without realizing it, my gloved hands were back on the controls. And I was chasing him again. Flying behind him, swooping when he swooped, trying to follow his every move.

*Powpowpow.* The ammo points rolled up. I had over 500,000 now.

Dr. Maniac stretched out his arms and flew away from the beach. The sound of the wind roared in my helmet. And suddenly, I heard bird sounds. Hoarse *caws* and cries.

And a swarm of fanged vampire seagulls rose up in front of me. Their wings raised high, they began to spit blood at me.

Each time I was hit, I FELT it! I knew this was just a game. But I *felt* every hit, every blast of the wind and the water!

On the screen, I dropped lower in the sky. A few

116

more hits, and I'd sink into the ocean! Would I feel myself *drowning*?

I raised the blaster. I aimed and started to shoot.

*POP!* A vampire seagull exploded on the screen in a flash of red and yellow.

*POP! POP!* I blasted two more.

"Ow!" I was hit again. The disgusting birds were *raining* blood on me.

I was sinking . . . sinking. . . . The tossing waves reached up to pull me down. And once again —

GAME OVER.

"Okay, I'm done!" I shouted. "You win!"

I struggled to catch my breath. I grabbed the sides of the helmet and started to pull it off.

"Hey!" It was stuck or something.

I grabbed the visor and tugged up on it. But the helmet didn't slide. Again, I pressed my gloved hands against the sides. I pushed up with all my strength.

No. The helmet had tightened itself to my head.

I decided I could remove it easier without the gloves. So I grabbed the fingers of one glove and pulled at them.

"Huh?" I let out a startled cry when the glove wouldn't slide, either.

Frantically, I pulled at one glove, then the other.

"I'm not crazy — I'm a MANIAC!"

117

Dr. Maniac's scream rang inside the helmet. On the big video screen, he laughed his evil laugh and took off again. This time, he was flying over a jungle.

My hands grabbed the control, and I guided myself after him.

"I . . . I can't QUIT!" I cried out loud. "It won't let me STOP!"

*Powpowpowpow!*

I rang up ammo points as I swooped and dove after the flying villain. And now we were flying in a wild path through the jungle trees.

My left hand frantically guided the controller. My right hand grabbed the blaster and began shooting at jungle animals as they leaped at me.

*Powpowpow!*

"I want to quit!" I cried. My voice was muffled by the helmet. Drowned out by the loud music, the screams of the jungle animals, and Dr. Maniac's insane laughter.

"I want to STOP!" I screamed.

The game ended.

I struggled to pull off the gloves. I clamped my teeth over a middle finger and tugged with all my might. No. The glove stuck to my hand.

With a furious cry, I grabbed the sides of the helmet and began twisting it one way, then the other. But that sent pain shooting down my neck. The helmet didn't budge.

118

Another game began. Dr. Maniac flew over a red-sand desert.

I grabbed the controller. I couldn't stop myself. I couldn't keep my hand from gripping it. I took off after him, his laughter ringing through the helmet.

Sweat poured down my forehead. My legs trembled. My heart raced.

The game ended. Another game started. Then another.

I bent over the game console, struggling to free myself. But I was trapped. I was a prisoner. A prisoner of a video game!

Another game started. We were racing across a big city again.

Suddenly, in the glass that covered the video screen, I saw a reflection. Someone stood behind me in the arcade room. I could see his shadowy figure in the glass.

I stared harder at the reflection. The figure stepped closer — and I realized it was Dr. Maniac!

Standing behind me?

Still gripping the controls, I spun my head around.

No. No one standing there.

I turned back to the game — and saw Dr. Maniac's grinning reflection in the glass.

I turned again and glanced around the room. No one there.

119

*Powpowpowpow!* The game continued. I was back in the subway tunnel, blasting away at the ugly underground monster.

My arms ached. My legs shook. My throat felt so dry, I couldn't swallow.

The game ended and another game began. I tried to free myself, but I was stuck.

And then I heard a noise behind me. I whipped my head around and saw two girls walk into the room. Carly Beth and Sabrina?

No. Two other girls. They looked about my age. They both had coppery red hair and brown eyes. One wore a red-and-yellow sundress. The other had a pale green T-shirt over white shorts. Were they sisters?

They stopped just past the doorway and stared at me.

"HELP ME!" I screamed. "Help! I'm stuck here!" I tried to point to the game machine, but my hands wouldn't let go of the controller and blaster.

They took a few steps closer.

"Please —" I begged. "It's no joke. It's for real. Help me!"

"What do you want us to do?" the one in the sundress asked.

"Pull the plug!" I shouted. "Unplug the machine! Hurry! Please! Unplug it!"

Dr. Maniac cackled in my ears. "I'm not crazy —

I'm a MANIAC!" he shrieked. And another game began.

"Unplug it! Unplug it!" I cried.

The girls ran to the back of the machine. They dropped to their knees to find the plug.

I couldn't see them. On the screen, I was flying over the ocean again. The vampire seagulls squawked and began to spit blood at me.

"Unplug it! Can you find the plug?" I cried. "Please —"

Both girls poked their heads up at the same time. "We *can't* unplug it," one of them shouted. "It isn't plugged in!"

One girl held up the plug. "See?!"

Dr. Maniac's laughter rang in the helmet. Vampire seagulls rained blood on me. I was sinking toward the ocean waves.

My arms ached. My chest throbbed. I could feel my legs about to cave in.

I'd played at least twenty games. I could barely see straight. But I couldn't stop myself. I leaned over the console, blasting away at the seagulls.

"Find the ON-OFF switch!" I cried. "Hurry!"

The girls circled the machine. They bent down and searched under the video screen and all around the base of the console.

"We can't find it!" one of them shouted.

"There's no switch!" the other one said. "We can't turn it off!"

*Powpowpow!*

*KA-BOOM!* A seagull exploded on the screen. Three more vicious birds came flying at me.

I let out a moan. Everything faded to gray, then

black. I could feel my eyes roll up in my head. And my knees buckle.

I knew I was fainting, but I couldn't stop myself.

My chest hit the front of the game console as I fell. And then sharp pain shot through my head as it hit the glass on the way down.

You know how they always show people seeing stars in comic books? They bang their heads on something and then they see stars floating above their heads?

Well, I really did see them. Bright gold ones twinkling against a black background. And then the stars faded, and I blacked out.

When I opened my eyes, I was flat on my back on the floor. Slowly, I lifted my head. I stared at the video screen. Blank. The game had finally stopped.

I sat up. I pulled off the helmet. "Yes!" I cried. "I'm *free*!"

I pulled off the gloves. I tossed them across the room.

The girls stood there gaping at me.

"I'm okay," I said. "It's lucky I've got a hard head. I fall down a lot."

I was trying to be funny, but they didn't laugh.

They moved forward quickly. They grabbed my arms and pulled me to my feet. "You have to come with us," the one in the sundress said. "It's not safe here."

They held my arms tightly and started to guide me to the door.

"Hurry. Just follow us," the other girl said.

"Whoa." I pulled my arms free. "Where are you taking me?"

"Away from here," the first one said. "Far away. Where it's safe."

"Huh? Excuse me?" I cried. "Who *are* you?"

"I'm Britney Crosby," the first girl said. "That's my friend Molly Molloy."

Britney and Molly? Where had I heard those names before?

"I'm Robby Schwartz," I said. "I —"

"Come on, Robby — hurry," Britney said. She grabbed my arm again. "HorrorLand isn't safe."

"Did you think getting stuck on that game was an accident?" Molly asked. "You just saw for yourself how dangerous it is here."

"Come with us," Britney said, pulling me through the arcade.

"But . . . where?" I asked again. These girls were definitely weird.

"To the Other Park," Molly said in a whisper. She glanced around to make sure no one overheard. "We'll be safe there."

"Huh? Other Park?" I cried.

"The special guests were all brought to HorrorLand for *revenge*," Britney said. She squeezed my arm. I could see she was frightened. "We have to rescue the others, too," she said.

"Revenge? Who would want revenge?" I demanded. "I don't understand what you're saying. You're not making any sense!"

The blue light of the arcade washed over us as they pulled me to the door. The games were quiet now. It was very late. The big room had emptied out.

"Just trust us," Molly said. "We have to bring you to the Other Park with us."

She pulled a token from her pocket. She raised it in front of my face.

The golden coin was so shiny and new, I could see my reflection on it. And I could see the words engraved on the front: PANIC PARK.

"Just look at this for a minute," Molly said.

I laughed. "Are you trying to hypnotize me?"

They didn't answer. And suddenly, as I gazed at the shiny golden token, I began to feel weird. I mean, *really* weird.

Like I was being pulled to the coin. Like being sucked into my own reflection by a powerful force.

I could feel my whole body floating off the floor, flying toward the coin in Molly's hand. As if I were weightless. As if I could disappear into the shiny token.

Closer . . . closer . . . I was melting. My body was shrinking, shrinking to fit into the golden circle. Shrinking away . . .

I took a deep breath and let out an angry scream. "NOOOO!"

With a burst of strength, I slapped the token out of Molly's hand.

She gasped, and we both watched it fly across the room. It came to a spinning stop in front of the arcade door.

"Get it!" Molly cried to her friend.

But before anyone could move, the door swung open.

"Hey!" I let out a startled cry.

A ventriloquist's dummy stood by itself in the doorway. No one holding him up. No one else around.

The dummy wore a tight-fitting gray suit with a red bow tie. It had a crazy smile on its painted lips, and its big eyes darted from side to side.

I turned and saw both Britney and Molly back away in horror.

"Slappy!" They screamed the name together.

I wanted to get away from these two girls. They were acting totally weird.

I started to the door. I planned to push the dummy out of my way.

But the thing started to *move*!

It took a few steps toward me — and stuck out its wooden hands to block my way.

"Hey!" I shouted. I turned back to Britney and Molly. "Who is making him walk?"

Before they could answer, the dummy *spoke*, in a hoarse, tinny, high voice: "Who made *you* so stupid? This isn't a staring contest! Pick up the token, Jerkface!"

The girls uttered frightened cries and started to back away.

"This is crazy!" I cried. "Who is making him talk?"

"Better do as he says," Britney murmured.

"PICK UP THE TOKEN!" the dummy shrieked. "Listen to your new *girlfriends*!"

I balled my hands into tight fists. I took a step toward the little guy.

"Robby — be careful!" Britney called. "He's *evil*!"

I glanced back. "You know him?"

"He . . . he followed us here!" Molly stammered. "His name is Slappy. He's alive. Really!"

"Yeah. For sure," I muttered. I spun around to face the dummy. "Get out of my way, Slappy!" I shouted.

Robby Schwartz, superhero, strikes again! I lowered my shoulder and hurtled at him, ready to bump him out of the doorway.

"OWWWW!" I howled in pain as he snapped his wooden jaws onto my ear.

I brought my head up and lifted the dummy off the floor. I swung my head around, trying to throw him off me.

But he clung to my ear. And his wooden lips clamped down tighter.

Pain shot through my head. I dropped to my knees. I grabbed the dummy with both hands. I shook him and struggled to pull him off.

"It . . . it won't let go!" I gasped. The pain was so intense, I could barely breathe. *"You're biting off my ear!"* I screamed.

Finally, the dummy let go. And then it spoke again: "Pick up the token, Britney."

Britney hesitated for a second. But she was too

frightened to disobey the dummy. She bent down and picked up the golden token.

"Hold it in front of this long-haired geek!" Slappy ordered.

Britney obeyed. She raised the token close to my face. It was so shiny that I could see my reflection.

And once again, I felt myself pulled toward it . . . floating off the floor and out of the room. Once again, I felt myself being dragged into the golden light of the token.

The light grew brighter . . . brighter . . . until I shut my eyes against it.

When I opened my eyes, I found myself sprawled on the floor of the arcade. Feeling dizzy and exhausted, I raised my head. "Britney? Molly?"

Instead, two other girls stared down at me. I squinted up at them.

"Robby, what is your problem?" Carly Beth asked. "Why are you sitting on the floor?"

"There's no time to play video games," Sabrina said. She grabbed one arm and helped pull me to my feet.

I shook my head, trying to force away the dizziness. "Where are the other two girls?" I asked. "And the dummy?"

Both girls glanced around the empty arcade. "There's no one else here," Carly Beth said.

"But they were here a second ago," I said. "They said the special guests aren't safe. That we have to leave."

Carly Beth stepped up to me and touched the side of my head. "What's that bump?" she asked. "Did you hit your head?"

I reached up and felt a lump. It hurt when I pressed it. "I banged it against a game machine," I said.

Sabrina laughed. "First you trip over a stuffed toy. Then you crash your head into a video game?"

"Listen to me," I said. "It isn't funny. The girls came to help me. They said we have to get out of HorrorLand. We have to get to the other park."

Carly Beth rolled her eyes. "There *were* no other girls," she said. "You hit your head, Robby. You knocked yourself out. You dreamed it."

"Come on. Let's go find the others," Sabrina said. She took my left arm. Carly Beth took my right. They began to lead me out of the arcade.

My mind spun. Were they right? Was it just a crazy dream? Did I dream that those two missing girls came to my rescue? They seemed so real. . . .

"Hey — stop!" I cried. I jerked my arms free. Just inside the door, I bent down and picked something up off the floor. . . .

The golden token.

To be continued in . . .

## #6 WHO'S YOUR MUMMY?

LUKE —
NO MORE CODENAMES.
NO MORE SECRETS.
IT'S TIME TO TELL EVERYBODY
OUR STORY SO WE CAN
WARN ROBBY SCHWARTZ AND THE
OTHERS. R U WITH ME?
I'LL CHECK THE SITE FOR
YOUR ANSWER!
YOUR SIS,
LIZZY

COMPOSITION

One Day at HorrorLand

Connects to Map #1

Connects to Map #3

Why do Luke and Lizzy
know so many secrets about
HorrorLand?
Before the Fear Files, they
starred in

## ONE DAY AT HORRORLAND

Turn the page for a peek at R.L. Stine's classic
prequel to the Goosebumps HorrorLand series.
Now available with exclusive new bonuses—
including a secret guide to EscapeHorrorLand.com
and other suprises!

As we entered the gates to HorrorLand, we had no idea that, in less than an hour, we would all be lying in our coffins.

I'm the calm one in the Morris family. Everyone says, "Lizzy, you're the calm one." And I'm trying to tell this story calmly.

But believe me — there's *no way*!

We had never planned to go to HorrorLand. In fact, we'd never heard of it.

The five of us were squeezed into Dad's little Toyota, on our way to spend the day at Zoo Gardens Theme Park. Dad had messed up and left the map at home. But Mom said the park would be real easy to find.

When we got close to the park, Mom said there would be lots of signs to direct us. But so far we hadn't seen a single sign.

Dad was driving, and Mom was beside him in the front. I was squeezed in back with my little brother Luke, who is ten, and Luke's friend Clay.

It wasn't the best place to be. My brother cannot sit still for a second. Especially in the car. He just has too much energy. And he's totally goofy.

The longer we drove, the more restless Luke became. He tried wrestling with Clay, but there really wasn't room. Then he tried arm wrestling with him, and the two of them kept bumping me until I lost my temper and started shouting at them to stop.

"Why don't you three play Alphabet?" Mom suggested from the front. "Look out the window for letters."

"There aren't any," Luke replied. "There aren't any signs."

"There isn't *anything* to look at," Clay grumbled.

He was right. We were driving past flat sandy fields. There were a few scraggly trees here and there. The rest was all desert.

"I'm going to take this turnoff," Dad announced. He took off his Chicago Cubs cap and scratched his thinning blond hair. "Haven't I already taken this turnoff?"

Dad is the only blond in the family. Mom, Luke, and I all have straight black hair and blue eyes.

In fact, Dad doesn't look as if he belongs in the same family. The three of us are tall and thin, with very fair skin. And Dad is short and kind of chubby, with a round face that's almost always pink. I tease him all the time because I think he looks a lot more like a wrestler than a bank manager, which he is.

"I'm pretty sure we've already been here," Dad said unhappily.

"It's hard to tell. It's all desert," Mom replied, gazing out her window.

"Very helpful," Dad muttered.

"How can I be helpful?" Mom shot back. "*You're* the one who left the map on the kitchen table."

"I thought you packed it," Dad grumbled.

"Why should it be my job to pack the map?" Mom cried.

"Break it up, you two," I interrupted. Once they start fighting, they never stop. It's always best to interrupt them quickly before they really get into it.

"I'm the Mad Pincher!" Luke cried. He let out a gruesome horror-movie laugh and started pinching Clay's ribs and arms.

I hate Luke's Mad Pincher routine more than anything. I was so glad that Clay was sitting in the middle next to Luke, and not me. Usually, the only way to stop Luke's pinching is to slug him.

Clay started squirming and laughing. He thinks everything Luke does is a riot. He laughs at all of my brother's stupid jokes and stunts. I think that's why Luke likes Clay so much.

The two of them began pinching each other. Then Luke shoved Clay into me. "Give me a break!" I cried.

I shoved Clay back. I know I shouldn't have. But it was getting hot in the car, and we'd been driving for hours, and what was I supposed to do?

"Lizzy! Boys! Chill out back there!" Dad cried.

"Dad, nobody says 'chill out' anymore," I told him calmly and quietly.

For some reason, that made him go berserk. He started yelling, and his face got bright red.

I knew he wasn't mad at me. He was mad because he couldn't find Zoo Gardens Theme Park.

"Everybody just take a deep breath and be silent," Mom suggested.

"Ow! Stop pinching me!" Clay screamed. He gave Luke a hard shove.

"*You* stop pinching *me!*" my brother shrieked, shoving him back.

Boys can really be animals.

"Hey, look — a sign up ahead!" Mom pointed as a large green sign came into view.

Luke and Clay stopped fighting. Dad leaned forward over the steering wheel, squinting through the windshield.

"Does it say where the park is?" Luke demanded.

"Does it say where we are?" Clay asked.

The words on the sign came into view as we drove past it. It said: SIGN FOR RENT.

We all let out disappointed groans.

"The Mad Pincher returns!" Luke cried. He gave Clay a hard pinch on the arm. Luke never knows when to quit.

"This road isn't going anywhere," Dad said, scowling. "I'll have to turn around and get back on the highway. If I can find it."

"I think you should ask someone for directions," Mom suggested.

"Ask someone? Ask someone?" Dad exploded. "Do you *see* anyone I can ask?" His face was bright red again. He drove with one hand so he could use the other to shake a fist.

"I meant if you see a gas station," Mom murmured.

"A gas station?" Dad screamed. "I don't even see a tree!"

Dad was right. I stared out the window and saw nothing but white sand on both sides of the road. The sun beamed down on it, making it gleam. The sand was so bright, it nearly looked like snow.

"I meant to go north," Dad muttered. "The desert is south. We must have gone south."

"You'd better turn around," Mom urged.

"Are we lost?" Clay asked. I could hear some fear in his voice.

Clay isn't the bravest kid in the world. In fact,

he is pretty easy to scare. Once I crept up behind him in our backyard at night and whispered his name — and he almost jumped right out of his shoes!

"Dad, are we lost?" Luke repeated the question.

"Yeah, we're lost," Dad replied quietly. "Hopelessly lost."

Clay let out a soft cry and slumped in the seat. He looked a little like a balloon deflating.

"Don't tell him that!" Mom cried sharply.

"What *should* I tell him?" Dad snapped back. "We're nowhere near Zoo Gardens. We're nowhere near civilization! We're in the desert, going nowhere!"

"Just turn around. I'm sure we'll find someone we can ask," Mom said softly. "And stop being so dramatic."

"We're all going to die in the desert," Luke said with a gruesome grin on his face. "And buzzards will peck out our eyeballs and eat our flesh."

My brother has a great sense of humor, doesn't he?

You can't imagine what it's like having to live with a total ghoul!

"Luke, stop scaring Clay," Mom said, turning in her seat to glare at Luke.

"I'm not scared," Clay insisted. But he looked scared.

## About the Author

R.L. Stine's books are read all over the world. So far, his books have sold more than 300 million copies, making him one of the most popular children's authors in history. Besides Goosebumps, R.L. Stine has written the teen series Fear Street and the funny series Rotten School, as well as the Mostly Ghostly series, The Nightmare Room series, and the two-book thriller *Dangerous Girls*. R.L. Stine lives in New York with his wife, Jane, and Minnie, his King Charles spaniel. You can learn more about him at www.RLStine.com.

# The Original Bone-Chilling Series

## Now with All-New Behind-the-Screams Author Interviews and More!

**◼ SCHOLASTIC**

**www.scholastic.com/goosebumps**

GBCLSC

# THE SCARIEST PLACE ON EARTH!

# EnterHorrorLand.com

# THIS BOOK IS YOUR TICKET TO

## www.EnterHorrorLand.com

## CHECKLIST #5

☑

- ☐ In the Werewolf Petting Zoo, the wolf cubs are locking guests in cages! Escape!

- ☐ Make your way through Wolfsbane Forest. But don't FUR-get the way out!

- ☐ Do you have what it takes to survive Dr. Maniac's video game? Play to find out!

- ☐ Defeat Dr. Maniac! Good luck!

An all-new, all-terrifying series from the master of fright!

**Goosebumps HorrorLand**

DR. MANIAC VS. ROBBY SCHWARTZ
R.L. STINE
SCHOLASTIC

☐

THE ORIGINAL SERIES FROM THE MASTER OF FRIGHT!

**Goosebumps**

ONE DAY at HORRORLAND
R.L. STINE
SCHOLASTIC

_____

**USER NAME**

_____

**PASSWORD**

NOW WITH
BONUS
FEATURES!

For more frights, check out the Goosebumps HorrorLand video game!
Screaming into stores October 2008.

■ SCHOLASTIC